THE LANDLADY

FYODOR DOSTOYEVSKY

A Digireads.com Book
Digireads.com Publishing

The Landlady
By Fyodor Dostoyevsky
Translated by Constance Garnett
ISBN 10: 1-4209-4057-0
ISBN 13: 978-1-4209-4057-2

Please visit *www.digireads.com*

THE LANDLADY

A STORY

PART I

I

Ordynov had made up his mind at last to change his lodgings. The landlady with whom he lodged, the poor and elderly widow of a petty functionary, was leaving Petersburg, for some reason or other, and setting off to a remote province to live with relations, before the first of the month when his time at his lodging was up. Staying on till his time was up the young man thought regretfully of his old quarters and felt vexed at having to leave them; he was poor and lodgings were dear. The day after his landlady went away, he took his cap and went out to wander about the back streets of Petersburg, looking at all the bills stuck up on the gates of the houses, and choosing by preference the dingiest and most populous blocks of buildings, where there was always more chance of finding a corner in some poor tenant's flat.

He had been looking for a long time, very carefully, but soon he was visited by new, almost unknown, sensations. He looked about him at first carelessly and absent-mindedly, then with attention, and finally with intense curiosity. The crowd and bustle of the street, the noise, the movement, the novelty of objects and the novelty of his position, all the paltry, everyday triviality of town life so wearisome to a busy Petersburger spending his whole life in the fruitless effort to gain by toil, by sweat and by various other means, a snug little home, in which to rest in peace and quiet,—all this vulgar prose and dreariness aroused in Ordynov, on the contrary, a sensation of gentle gladness and serenity. His pale cheeks began to be suffused with a faint flush, his eyes began to shine as though with new hope, and he drew deep and eager breaths of the cold fresh air. He felt unusually lighthearted.

He always led a quiet and absolutely solitary life. Three years before, after taking his degree and becoming to a great extent his own master, he went to see an old man whom he had known only at second-hand, and was kept waiting a long while before the liveried servants consented to take his name in a second time. Then he walked into a dark, lofty, and deserted room, one of those dreary-looking rooms still to be found in old-fashioned family mansions that have been spared by time, and saw in it a grey-headed old man, hung with orders of distinction, who had been the friend and colleague of his father, and was his guardian. The old man handed him a tiny screw of notes. It turned out to be a very small sum: it was all that was left of his ancestral estates, which had been sold by auction pay the family debts. Ordynov accepted his inheritance unconcernedly, took leave for ever of his guardian, and went out into the street. It was a cold, gloomy, autumn evening; the young man was dreamy and his heart was torn with a sort of unconscious sadness. There was a glow of fire in his eyes; he felt feverish, and was hot and chilly by turns. He calculated on the way that on his money he could live for two or three years, or even on half rations for four years. It grew dusk and began to drizzle with rain. He had taken the first corner he came across and within an hour had moved into it. There he shut himself up as though he were in a monastery, as though he had renounced the world. Within two years he had become a complete recluse.

He had grown shy and unsociable without being aware of the fact; meanwhile, it never occurred to him that there was another sort of life—full of noise and uproar, of continual excitement, of continual variety, which was inviting him and was sooner or later inevitable. It is true that he could not avoid hearing of it, but he had never known it or sought to know it: from childhood his life had been exceptional; and now it was more exceptional than ever. He was devoured by the deepest and most insatiable passion, which absorbs a man's whole life and does not, for beings like Ordynov, provide any niche in the domain of practical daily activity. This passion was science. Meanwhile it was consuming his youth, marring his rest at nights with its slow, intoxicating poison, robbing him of wholesome food and of fresh air which never penetrated to his stifling corner. Yet, intoxicated by his passion, Ordynov refused to notice it. He was young and, so far, asked for nothing more. His passion made him a babe as regards external existence and totally incapable of forcing other people to stand aside when needful to make some sort of place for himself among them. Some clever people's science is a capital in their hands; for Ordynov it was a weapon turned against himself.

He was prompted rather by an instinctive impulse than by a logical, clearly defined motive for studying and knowing, and it was the same in every other work he had done hitherto, even the most trivial. Even as a child he had been thought queer and unlike his schoolfellows. He had never known his parents; he had to put up with coarse and brutal treatment from his schoolfellows, provoked by his odd and unsociable disposition, and that made him really unsociable and morose, and little by little he grew more and more secluded in his habits. But there never had been and was not even now any order and system in his solitary studies; even now he had only the first ecstasy, the first fever, the first delirium of the artist. He was creating a system for himself, it was being evolved in him by the years; and the dim, vague, but marvellously soothing image of an idea, embodied in a new, clarified form, was gradually emerging in his soul. And this form craved expression, fretting his soul; he was still timidly aware of its originality, its truth, its independence: creative genius was already showing, it was gathering strength and taking shape. But the moment of embodiment and creation was still far off, perhaps very far off, perhaps altogether impossible!

Now he walked about the streets like a recluse, like a hermit who has suddenly come from his dumb wilderness into the noisy, roaring city. Everything seemed to him new and strange. But he was so remote from all the world that was surging and clattering around him that he did not wonder at his own strange sensation. He seemed unconscious of his own aloofness; on the contrary, there was springing up in his heart a joyful feeling, a sort of intoxication, like the ecstasy of a hungry man who has meat and drink set before him after a long fast; though, of course, it was strange that such a trivial novelty as a change of lodgings could excite and thrill any inhabitant of Petersburg, even Ordynov; but the truth is that it had scarcely ever happened to him to go out with a practical object.

He enjoyed wandering about the streets more and more. He stared about at everything like a *flâneur*.

But, even now, inconsequent as ever, he was reading significance in the picture that lay so brightly before him, as though between the lines of a book. Everything struck him; he did not miss a single impression, and looked with thoughtful eyes into the faces of passing people, watched the characteristic aspect of everything around him and listened lovingly to the speech of the people as though verifying in everything the conclusions that had been formed in the stillness of solitary nights. Often some trifle impressed him, gave rise to an idea, and for the first time he felt vexed that he had so buried himself alive in his cell. Here everything moved more swiftly, his pulse was full and rapid, his mind, which had been oppressed by solitude and had been stirred and uplifted only by strained, exalted activity, worked now swiftly, calmly and boldly. Moreover, he had an unconscious longing to squeeze himself somehow into this life which was so strange to him, of which he had hitherto known—or rather correctly divined—only by the instinct of the artist. His heart began instinctively throbbing with a yearning for love and sympathy. He looked more attentively at the people who passed by him; but they were strangers, preoccupied and absorbed in thought, and by degrees Ordynov's careless lightheartedness began unconsciously to pass away; reality began to weigh upon him, and to inspire in him a sort of unconscious dread and awe. He began to be weary from the surfeit of new impressions, like an invalid who for the first time joyfully gets up from his sick bed, and sinks down giddy and stupefied by the movement and exhausted by the light, the glare, the whirl of life, the noise and medley of colours in the crowd that flutters by him. He began to feel dejected and miserable, he began to be full of dread for his whole life, for his work, and even for the future. A new idea destroyed his peace. A thought suddenly occurred to him that all his life he had been solitary and no one had loved him— and, indeed, he had succeeded in loving no one either. Some of the passers-by, with whom he had chanced to enter into conversation at the beginning of his walk, had looked at him rudely and strangely. He saw that they took him for a madman or a very original, eccentric fellow, which was indeed, perfectly correct. He remembered that every one was always somewhat ill at ease in his presence, that even in his childhood every one had avoided him on account of his dreamy, obstinate character, that sympathy for people had always been difficult and oppressive to him, and had been unnoticed by others, for though it existed in him there was no moral equality perceptible in it, a fact which had worried him even as a child, when he was utterly unlike other children of his own age. Now he remembered and reflected that always, at all times, he had been left out and passed over by every one.

Without noticing it, he had come into an end of Petersburg remote from the centre of the town. Dining after a fashion in a solitary restaurant, he went out to wander about again. Again he passed through many streets and squares. After them stretched long fences grey, and yellow; he began to come across quite dilapidated little cottages, instead of wealthy houses, and cried with them colossal factories, monstrous, soot-begrimed, red buildings with long chimneys. All round it was deserted and desolate, everything looked grim and forbidding, so at least it seemed to Ordynov. It was by now evening. He came out of a long side-street into a square where there stood a parish church.

He went into it without thinking. The service was just over, the church was almost empty, only two old women were kneeling near the entrance. The verger, a grey-headed old man, was putting out the candles. The rays of the setting sun were streaming down from above through a narrow window in the cupola and flooding one of the chapels with a sea of brilliant light, but it grew fainter and fainter, and the blacker the darkness that gathered under the vaulted roof, the more brilliantly glittered in places the gilt ikons, reflecting the flickering glow of the lamps and the lights. In an access of profound depression and some stifled feeling Ordynov leaned against the wall in the darkest corner of the church, and for an instant sank into forgetfulness. He came to himself when the even, hollow sound of the footsteps of two persons resounded in the building. He raised his eyes and an indescribable curiosity took possession of him at the sight of the two advancing figures. They were an old man and a young woman. The old man was tall, still upright and hale looking, but thin and of a sickly pallor. From his appearance he might have been taken for a merchant from some distant province. He was wearing a long black full-skirted coat trimmed with fur, evidently a holiday dress, and he wore it unbuttoned; under it could be seen some other long-skirted Russian garment, buttoned closely from top to bottom. His bare neck was covered with a bright red handkerchief carelessly knotted; in his hands he held a fur cap. His thin, long, grizzled beard fell down to his chest, and fiery, feverishly glowing eyes flashed a haughty, prolonged stare from under his frowning, overhanging brows. The woman was about twenty and wonderfully beautiful. She wore a splendid blue, fur-trimmed jacket, and her head was covered with a white satin kerchief tied under her chin. She walked with her eyes cast down, and a sort of melancholy dignity pervaded her whole figure and was vividly and mournfully reflected in the sweet contours of the childishly soft, mild lines of her face. There was something strange in this surprising couple.

The old man stood still in the middle of the church, and bowed to all the four points of the compass, though the church was quite empty; his companion did the same. Then he took her by the hand and led her up to the big ikon of the Virgin, to whom the church was dedicated. It was shining on the altar, with the dazzling light of the candles reflected on the gold and precious stones of the setting. The church verger, the last one remaining in the church, bowed respectfully to the old man, the latter nodded to him. The woman fell on her face, before the ikon. The old man took the hem of the veil that hung at the pedestal of the ikon and covered her head. A muffled sob echoed through the church.

Ordynov was impressed by the solemnity of this scene and waited in impatience for its conclusion. Two minutes later the woman raised her head and again the bright light of the lamp fell on her charming face. Ordynov started and took a step forward. She had already given her hand to the old man and they both walked quietly out of the church. Tears were welling up from her dark blue eyes under the long eyelashes that glistened against the milky pallor of her face, and were rolling down her pale cheeks. There was a glimpse of a smile on her lips; but there were traces in her face of some childlike fear and mysterious horror. She pressed timidly close to the old man and it could be seen that she was trembling from emotion.

Overwhelmed, tormented by a sweet and persistent feeling that was novel to him, Ordynov followed them quickly and overtook them in the church porch. The old man looked at him with unfriendly churlishness; she glanced at him, too, but absentmindedly, without curiosity, as though her mind were absorbed by some far-away thought. Ordynov followed them without understanding his own action. By now it had grown quite dark; he followed at a little distance. The old man and the young woman turned into a long, wide, dirty street full of hucksters' booths, corn chandlers' shops and taverns, leading straight to the city gates, and turned from it into a long narrow lane, with long fences on each side of it, running alongside the huge, blackened wall of a four-storeyed block of buildings, by the gates of which one could pass into another street also big and crowded. They were approaching the house; suddenly the old man turned round and looked with impatience at Ordynov. The young man stood still as though he had been shot; he felt himself how strange his impulsive conduct was. The old man looked round once more, as though he wanted to assure himself that his menacing gaze, had produced its effect, and then the two of them, he and the young woman, went in at the narrow gate of the courtyard. Ordynov turned back.

He was in the most discontented humour and was vexed with himself, reflecting that he had wasted his day, that he had tired himself for nothing, and had ended foolishly by magnifying into an adventure an incident that was absolutely ordinary.

However severe he had been with himself in the morning for his recluse habits, yet it was instinctive with him to shun anything that might distract him, impress and shock him in his external, not in his internal, artistic world. Now he thought mournfully and regretfully of his sheltered corner; then he was overcome by depression and anxiety about his unsettled position and the exertions before him. At last, exhausted and incapable of putting two ideas together, he made his way late at night to his lodging and realized with amazement that he had been about to pass the house in which he lived. Dumbfoundered, he shook his head, and put down his absented-mindedness to fatigue and, going up the stairs, at last reached his garret under the roof. There he lighted a candle—and a minute later the image of the weeping woman rose vividly before his imagination. So glowing, so intense was the impression, so longingly did his heart reproduce those mild, gentle features, quivering with mysterious emotion and horror, and bathed in tears of ecstasy or childish penitence, that there was a mist before his eyes and a thrill of fire seemed to run through all his limbs. But the vision did not last long. After enthusiasm, after ecstasy came reflection, then vexation, then impotent anger; without undressing he threw himself on his hard bed . . .

Ordynov woke up rather late in the morning, in a nervous, timid and oppressed state of mind. He hurriedly got ready, almost forcing himself to concentrate his mind on the practical problems before him, and set off in the opposite direction from that he had taken on his pilgrimage the day before. At last he found a lodging, a little room in the flat of a poor German called Schpies, who lived alone with a daughter called Tinchen. On receiving a deposit Schpies instantly took down the notice that was nailed on the gate to attract lodgers, complimented Ordynov on his devotion to science, and promised to work with him zealously himself. Ordynov said that he would move in in the evening. From there he was going home, but changed his mind and turned off in the other direction; his self-confidence returned and he smiled at his own curiosity. In his impatience the way seemed very long to him. At last he reached the church in which he had been the evening before. Evening service was going on. He chose a place from which he could see almost all the congregation; but the figures he was looking for were not there. After waiting a long time he went away, blushing. Resolutely suppressing in himself an involuntary feeling, he tried obstinately to force himself, to change the current of his thoughts. Reflecting on everyday practical matters, he remembered he had not had dinner and, feeling that he was hungry, he went into the same tavern in which he had dined the day before. Unconsciously he sauntered a long lime about the streets, through crowded and deserted alleys, and at last came out into a desolate region where the town ended in a vista of fields that were turning yellow; he came to himself when the deathlike silence struck him by its strangeness and unfamiliarity. It was a dry and frosty day such as are frequent in Petersburg in October. Not far away was a cottage; and near it stood two haystacks; a little horse with prominent ribs was standing unharnessed, with drooping head and lip thrust out, beside a little two-wheeled gig, and seemed to be pondering over something. A watch-dog, growling, gnawed a bone beside a broken wheel, and a child of three who, with nothing on but his shirt, was engaged in combing his shaggy white head, stared in wonder at the solitary stranger from the town. Behind the cottage there was a stretch of field and cottage garden. There was a dark patch of forest against the blue sky on the horizon, and on the opposite side were thick snowclouds, which seemed chasing before them a flock of flying birds moving noiselessly one after another across the sky. All was still and, as it were, solemnly melancholy, full of a palpitating, hidden suspense . . . Ordynov was walking on further and further, but the desolation weighed upon him. He turned back to the town, from which there suddenly floated the deep clamour of bells, ringing for evening service; he redoubled his pace and within a short time he was again entering the church that had been so familiar to him since the day before.

The unknown woman was there already. She was kneeling at the very entrance, among the crowd of worshippers. Ordynov forced his way through the dense mass of beggars, old women in rags, sick people and cripples, who were waiting for alms at the church door, and knelt down beside the stranger. His clothes touched her clothes and he heard the breath that came irregularly from her lips as she whispered a fervent prayer. As before, her features were quivering with a feeling of boundless devotion, and tears again were falling and drying on her burning cheeks, as though washing away some fearful crime. It was quite dark in the place where they were both kneeling, and only from time to time the dim flame of the lamp, flickering in the draught from the narrow open window pane, threw a quivering glimmer on her face, every feature of which printed itself on the young man's memory, making his eyes swim, and rending his heart with a vague, insufferable pain. But this torment had a peculiar, intense ecstacy of its own. At last he could not endure it; his breast began shuddering and aching all in one instant with a sweet and unfamiliar yearning, and, bursting into sobs, he bowed down with his feverish head to the cold pavement of the church. He saw nothing and felt nothing but the ache in his heart, which thrilled with sweet anguish.

This extreme impressionability, sensitiveness, and lack of resisting power may have been developed by solitude, or this impulsiveness of heart may have been evolved in the exhausting, suffocating and hopeless silence of long, sleepless nights, in the midst of unconscious yearnings and impatient stirrings of spirit, till it was ready at last to explode and find an outlet, or it may have been simply that the time for that solemn moment had suddenly arrived and it was as inevitable as when on a sullen, stifling day the whole sky grows suddenly black and a storm pours rain and fire on the parched earth, hangs pearly drops on the emerald twigs, beats down the grass, the crops, crushes to the earth the tender cups of the flowers, in order that afterwards, at the first rays of the sun, everything, reviving again, may shine and rise to meet it, and triumphantly lift to the sky its sweet, luxuriant incense, glad and rejoicing in its new life . . .

But Ordynov could not think now what was the matter with him. He was scarcely conscious.

He hardly noticed how the service ended, and only recovered his senses as he threaded his way after his unknown lady through the crowd that thronged the entrance. At times he met her clear and wondering eyes. Stopped every minute by the people passing out, she turned round to him more than once; he could see that her surprise grew greater and greater, and all at once she flushed a fiery red. At that minute the same old man came forward again out of the crowd and took her by the arm. Ordynov met his morose and sarcastic stare again, and a strange anger suddenly gripped his heart. At last he lost sight of them in the darkness; then, with a superhuman effort, he pushed forward and got out of the church. But the fresh evening air could not restore him; his breathing felt oppressed and stifled, and his heart began throbbing slowly and violently as though it would have burst his breast. At last he saw that he really had lost his strangers—they were neither in the main street nor in the alley. But already a thought had come to Ordynov, and in his mind was forming one of those strange, decisive projects, which almost always succeed when they are carried out, in spite of their wildness. At eight o'clock next morning he went to the house from the side of the alley and walked into a narrow, filthy, and unclean backyard which was like an open cesspool in a house. The porter, who was doing something in the yard, stood still, leaned with his chin on the handle of his spade, looked Ordynov up and down and asked him what he wanted. The porter was a little fellow about five and twenty, a Tatar with an extremely old-looking face, covered with wrinkles.

"I'm looking for a lodging," Ordynov answered, impatiently.

"Which?" asked the porter, with a grin. He looked at Ordynov as if he knew all about him.

"I want a furnished room in a flat," answered Ordynov.

"There's none in that yard," the porter answered enigmatically.

"And here?"

"None here, either." The porter took up his spade again.

"Perhaps they will let me have one," said Ordynov, giving the porter ten kopecks.

The Tatar glanced at Ordynov, took the ten kopecks, then took up his spade again, and after a brief silence announced that: "No, there was no lodging." But the young man did not hear him; he walked along the rotten, shaking planks that lay in the pool towards the one entrance from that yard into the lodge of the house, a black, filthy, muddy entrance that looked as though it were drowning in the pool. In the lower storey lived a poor coffin-maker. Passing by his cheering workshop, Ordynov clambered by a half-broken, slippery, spiral staircase to the upper storey, felt in the darkness a heavy, clumsy door covered with rags of sacking, found the latch and opened it. He was not mistaken. Before him stood the same old man looking at him intently with extreme surprise.

"What do you want?" he asked abruptly and almost in whisper.

"Is there a room to let?" asked Ordynov, almost forgetting everything he had meant to say. He saw over the old man's shoulder the young woman.

The old man began silently closing the door, shutting Ordynov out.

"We have a lodging to let," the young woman's friendly voice said suddenly.

The old man let go of the door.

"I want a corner," said Ordynov, hurriedly entering the room and addressing himself to the beautiful woman.

But he stopped in amazement as though petrified, looking at his future landlord and landlady; before his eyes a mute and amazing scene was taking place. The old man was as pale as death, as though on the point of losing consciousness. He looked at the woman with a leaden, fixed, searching gaze. She too, grew pale at first; then blood rushed to her face and her eyes flashed strangely. She led Ordynov into another little room.

The whole flat consisted of one rather large room, divided into three by two partitions. From the outer room they went straight into a narrow dark passage; directly opposite was the door, evidently leading to a bedroom the other side of the partition. On the right, the other side of the passage, they went into the room which was to let; it was narrow and pokey, squeezed in between the partition and two low windows; it was blocked up with the objects necessary for daily life; it was poor and cramped but passably clean. The furniture consisted of a plain white table, two plain chairs and a locker that ran both sides of the wall. A big, old-fashioned ikon in a gilt wreath stood over a shelf in a corner and a lamp was burning before it. There was a huge, clumsy Russian stove partly in this room and partly in the passage. It was clear that it was impossible for three people to live in such a flat.

They began discussing terms but incoherently and hardly understanding one another. Two paces away from her, Ordynov could hear the beating of her heart; he saw she was trembling with emotion and, it seemed, with fear. At last they came to an agreement of some sort. The young man announced that he would move in at once and glanced at his landlord. The old man was standing at the door, still pale, but a quiet, even dreamy smile had stolen on to his lips. Meeting Ordynov's eyes he frowned again.

"Have you a passport?" he asked suddenly, in a loud and abrupt voice, opening the door into the passage for him.

"Yes," answered Ordynov, suddenly taken aback.

"Who are you?"

"Vassily Ordynov, nobleman, not in the service, engaged in private work," he answered, falling into the old man's tone.

"So am I," answered the old man. "I'm Ilya Murin, artisan. Is that enough for you? You can go . . ."

An hour later Ordynov was in his new lodging, to the surprise of himself and of his German who, together with his dutiful Tinchen was beginning to suspect that his new lodger had deceived him.

Ordynov did not understand how it had all happened, and he did not want to understand . .

II

His heart was beating so violently that he was giddy, and everything was green before his eyes; mechanically he busied himself arranging his scanty belongings in his new lodgings: he undid the bag containing various necessary possessions, opened the box containing his books and began laying them out on the table; but soon all this work dropped from his hands. Every minute there rose before his eyes the image of the woman, the meeting with whom had so troubled and disturbed his whole existence, who had filled his heart with such irresistible, violent ecstasy—and such happiness seemed at once flooding his starved life that his thoughts grew dizzy and his soul swooned in anguish and perplexity.

He took his passport and carried it to the landlord in the hope of getting a glance at her. But Murin scarcely opened the door; he took the paper from him, said, "Good; live in peace," and closed the door again. An unpleasant feeling came over Ordynov. He did not know why, but it was irksome for him to look at the old man. There was something spiteful and contemptuous in his eyes. But the unpleasant impression quickly passed off. For the last three days Ordynov had, in comparison with his former stagnation, been living in a whirl of life; but he could not reflect, he was, indeed, afraid to. His whole existence was in a state of upheaval and chaos; he dimly felt as though his life had been broken in half; one yearning, one expectation possessed him, and no other thoughts troubled him.

In perplexity he went back to his room. There by the stove in which the cooking was done a little humpbacked old woman was busily at work, so filthy and clothed in such rags that she was a pitiful sight. She seemed very ill-humoured and grumbled to herself at times, mumbling with her lips. She was his landlord's servant. Ordynov tried to talk to her, but she would not speak, evidently from ill-humour. At last dinner-time arrived. The old woman took cabbage soup, pies and beef out of the oven, and took them to her master and mistress. She gave some of the same to Ordynov. After dinner there was a deathlike silence in the flat.

Ordynov took up a book and spent a long time turning over its pages, trying to follow the meaning of what he had read often before. Losing patience, he threw down the book and began again putting his room to rights; at last he took up his cap, put on his coat and went out into the street. Walking at hazard, without seeing the road, he still tried as far as he could to concentrate his mind, to collect his scattered thoughts and to reflect a little upon his position. But the effort only reduced him to misery, to torture. He was attacked by fever and chills alternately, and at times his heart beat so violently that he had to support himself against the wall. "No, better death," he thought; "better death," he whispered with feverish, trembling lips, hardly thinking of what he was saying. He walked for a very long time; at last, feeling that he was soaked to the skin and noticing for the first time that it was pouring with rain, he returned home. Not far from home he saw his porter. He fancied that the Tatar stared at him for some time with curiosity, and then went his way when he noticed that he had been seen.

"Good-morning," said Ordynov, overtaking him. "What are you called?"

"Folks call me porter," he answered, grinning.

"Have you been porter here long?"

"Yes."

"Is my landlord an artisan?"

"Yes, if he says so."

"What does he do?"

"He's ill, lives, prays to God. That's all."

"Is that his wife?"

"What wife?"

"Who lives with him."

"Ye-es, if he says so. Good-bye, sir."

The Tatar touched his cap and went off to his den.

Ordynov went to his room. The old woman, mumbling and grumbling to herself, opened the door to him, fastened it again with the latch, and again climbed on the stove where she spent her life. It was already getting dark. Ordynov was going to get a light, when he noticed that the door to the landlord's room was locked. He called the old woman, who, propping herself on her elbow, looked sharply at him from the stove, as though wondering what he wanted with the landlord's lock; she threw him a box of matches without a word. He went back into his room and again, for the hundredth time, tried to busy himself with his books and things. But, little by little without understanding what he was doing, he sat down on the locker, and it seemed to him that he fell asleep. At times he came to himself and realized that his sleep was not sleep but the agonizing unconsciousness of illness. He heard a knock at the door, heard it opened, and guessed that it was the landlord and landlady returning from evening service. At that point it occurred to him that he must go in to them for something. He stood up, and it seemed to him that he was already going to them, but stumbled and fell over a heap of firewood which the old woman had flung down in the middle of the floor. At that point he lost consciousness completely, and opening his eyes after a long, long time, noticed with surprise that he was lying on the same locker, just as he was, in his clothes, and that over him there bent with tender solicitude a woman's face, divinely beautiful and, it seemed, drenched with gentle, motherly tears. He felt her put a pillow under his head and lay something warm over him, and some tender hand was laid on his feverish brow. He wanted to say "Thank you," he wanted to take that hand, to press it to his parched lips, to wet it with his tears, to kiss, to kiss it to all eternity. He wanted to say a great deal, but what he did not know himself; he would have been glad to die at that instant. But his arms felt like lead and would not move; he was as it were numb, and felt nothing but the blood pulsing through his veins, with throbs which seemed to lift him up as he lay in bed. Somebody gave him water. . . . At last he fell into unconsciousness.

He woke up at eight o'clock in the morning. The sunshine was pouring through the green, mouldy windows in a sheaf of golden rays; a feeling of comfort relaxed the sick man's limbs. He was quiet and calm, infinitely happy. It seemed to him that some one had just been by his pillow. He woke up, looking anxiously around him for that unseen being; he so longed to embrace his friend and for the first time in his life to say, "A happy day to you, my dear one."

"What a long time you have been asleep!" said a woman's, gentle voice.

Ordynov looked round, and the face of his beautiful landlady was bending over him with a friendly smile as clear as sunlight.

"How long you have been ill!" she said. "It's enough; get up. Why keep yourself in bondage? Freedom is sweeter than bread, fairer than sunshine. Get up, my dove, get up."

Ordynov seized her hand and pressed it warmly. It seemed to him that he was still dreaming.

"Wait; I've made tea for you. Do you want some tea? You had better have some; you'll be better. I've been ill myself and I know."

"Yes, give me something to drink," said Ordynov in a faint voice, and he got up on his feet. He was still very weak. A chill ran down his spine, all his limbs ached and felt as though they were broken. But there was a radiance in his heart, and the sunlight seemed to warm him with a sort of solemn, serene joy. He felt that a new, intense, incredible life was beginning for him. His head was in a slight whirl.

"Your name is Vassily?" she asked. "Either I have made a mistake, or I fancy the master called you that yesterday."

"Yes, it is. And what is your name?" said Ordynov, going nearer to her and hardly able to stand on his feet. He staggered.

She caught him by the arm, and laughed.

"My name is Katerina," she said, looking into his face with her large, clear blue eyes. They were holding each other by the hands.

"You want to say something to me," she said at last.

"I don't know," answered Ordynov; everything was dark before his eyes.

"See what a state you're in. There, my dove, there; don't grieve, don't pine; sit here at the table in the sun; sit quiet, and don't follow me," she added, seeing that the young man made a movement as though to keep her. "I will be with you again at once; you have plenty of time to see as much as you want of me." A minute later she brought in the tea, put it on the table, and sat down opposite him.

"Come, drink it up," she said. "Does your head ache?"

"No, now it doesn't ache," he said. "I don't know, perhaps it does. . . . I don't want any . . . enough, enough! . . . I don't know what's the matter with me," he said, breathless, and finding her hand at last. "Stay here, don't go away from me; give me your hand again. . . . It's all dark before my eyes; I look at you as though you were the sun," he said, as it were tearing the words out of his heart, and almost swooning with ecstasy as he uttered them. His throat was choking with sobs.

"Poor fellow! It seems you have not lived with anyone kind. You are all lonely and forlorn. Haven't you any relations?"

"No, no one; I am alone . . . never mind, it's no matter! Now it's better; I am all right now," said Ordynov, as though in delirium. The room seemed to him to be going round.

"I, too, have not seen my people for many years. You look at me as . . ." she said, after a minute's silence.

"Well . . . what?"

"You look at me as though my eyes were warming you! You know, when you love any one . . . I took you to my heart from the first word. If you are ill I will look after you again. Only don't you be ill; no. When you get up we will live like brother and sister. Will you? You know it's difficult to get a sister if God has not given you one."

"Who are you? Where do you come from?" said Ordynov in a weak voice.

"I am not of these parts. . . . You know folks tell how twelve brothers lived in a dark forest, and how a fair maiden lost her way in that forest. She went to them and tidied everything in the house for them, and put her love into everything. The brothers came home, and learned that the sister had spent the day there. They began calling her; she came out to them. They all called her sister, gave her freedom, and she was equal with all. Do you know the fairy tale?"

"I know it," whispered Ordynov.

"Life is sweet; is it sweet to you to live in the world?"

"Yes, yes; to live for a long time, to live for ages," answered Ordynov.

"I don't know," said Katerina dreamily." I should like death, too. Is life sweet? To love, and to love good people, yes. . . . Look, you've turned as white as flour again."

"Yes, my head's going round. . . ."

"Stay, I will bring you my bedclothes and another pillow; I will make up the bed here. Sleep, and dream of me; your weakness will pass. Our old woman is ill, too."

While she talked she began making the bed, from time to time looking at Ordynov with a smile.

"What a lot of books you've got!" she said, moving away a box.

She went up to him, took him by the right arm, led him to the bed, tucked him up and covered him with the quilt.

"They say books spoil a man," she said, shaking her head thoughtfully. "Do you like reading?"

"Yes,'" answered Ordynov, not knowing whether he were asleep or awake, and pressing Katerina's hand tight to assure himself that he was awake.

"My master has a lot of books; you should see! He says I they are religious books. He's always reading to me out of them. I will show you afterwards; you shall tell me afterwards what he reads to me out of them."

"Tell me," whispered Ordynov, keeping his eyes fixed on her.

"Are you fond of praying?" she said to him after a moment's silence. "Do you know, I'm afraid, I am always afraid . . ."

She did not finish; she seemed to be meditating. At last Ordynov raised his hand to her lips.

"Why are you kissing my hand?" (and her cheeks flushed faintly crimson). "Here, kiss them," she said, laughing and holding out both hands to him; then she took one away and laid it on his burning forehead; then she began to stroke and arrange his hair. She flushed more and more; at last she sat down on the floor by his bedside and laid her cheek against his cheek; her warm, damp breath tickled his face. . . . At last Ordynov felt a gush of hot tears fall from her eyes like molten lead on his cheeks. He felt weaker and weaker; he was too faint to move a hand. At that moment there was a knock at the door, followed by the grating of the bolt. Ordynov could hear the old man, his landlord, come in from the other side of the partition. Then he heard Katerina get up, without haste and without listening, take her books; he felt her make the sign of the cross over him as she went out; he closed his eyes. Suddenly a long, burning kiss scorched his feverish lips; it was like a knife thrust into his heart. He uttered a faint shriek and sank into unconsciousness . . .

Then a strange life began for him.

In moments when his mind was not clear, the thought flashed upon him that he was condemned to live in a long, unending dream, full of strange, fruitless agitations, struggles and sufferings. In terror he tried to resist the disastrous fatalism that weighed upon him, and at a moment of tense and desperate conflict some unknown force struck him again and he felt clearly that he was once more losing memory, that an impassable, bottomless abyss was opening before him and he was flinging himself into it with a wail of anguish and despair. At times he had moments of insufferable, devastating happiness, when the life force quickens convulsively in the whole organism, when the past shines clear, when the present glad moment resounds with triumph and one dreams, awake, of a future beyond all ken; when a hope beyond words falls with life-giving dew the soul; when one wants to scream with ecstasy; when one feels that the flesh is too weak for such a mass of impressions, that the whole thread of existence is breaking, and yet, at the same time, one greets all one's life with hope and renewal. At times he sank into lethargy, and then everything that had happened to him the last few days was repeated again, and passed across his mind in a swarm of broken, vague images; but his visions came in strange and enigmatic form. At times the sick man forgot what had happened to him, and wondered that he was not in his old lodging with his old landlady. He could not understand why the old woman did not come as she always used at the twilight hour to the stove, which from time to time flooded the whole dark corner of the room with a faint, flickering glow, to warm her trembling, bony hands at the dying embers before the fire went out, always talking and whispering to herself, and sometimes looking at him, her strange lodger, who had, she thought, grown mad by sitting so long over his books.

Another time he would remember that he had moved into another lodging; but how it had happened, what was the matter with him, and why he had to move he did not know, though his whole soul was swooning in continual, irresistible yearning. . . . But to what end, what led him on and tortured him, and who had kindled this terrible flame that stifled him and consumed his blood, again he did not know and could not remember. Often he greedily clutched at some shadow, often he heard the rustle of light footsteps near his bed, and a whisper, sweet as music, of tender, caressing words. Some one's moist and uneven breathing passed over his face, thrilling his whole being with love; hot tears dropped upon his feverish cheeks, and suddenly a long, tender kiss was printed on his lips; then his life lay languishing in unquenchable torture; all existence, the whole world, seemed standing still, seemed to be dying for ages around him, and everything seemed shrouded in a long night of a thousand years. . . .

Then the tender, calmly flowing years of early childhood seemed coming back to him again with serene joy, with the inextinguishable happiness, the first sweet wonder of life with the swarms of bright spirits that fluttered under every flower he picked, that sported with him on the luxuriant green meadow before the little house among the acacias, that smiled at him from the immense crystal lake beside which he would sit for hours together, listening to the splashing of the waves, and that rustled about him with their wings, lovingly scattering bright rainbow dreams upon his little cot, while his mother, bending over him, made the sign of the cross, kissed him, and sang him sweet lullabies in the long, peaceful nights. But then a being suddenly began to appear who overwhelmed him with a childlike terror, first bringing into his life the slow poison of sorrow and tears; he dimly felt that an unknown old man held all his future years in thrall, and, trembling, he could not turn his eyes away from him. The wicked old man followed him about everywhere. He peeped out and treacherously nodded to the boy from under every bush in the copse, laughed and mocked at him, took the shape of every doll, grimacing and laughing in his hands, like a spiteful evil gnome: he set every one of the child's inhuman schoolfellows against him, or, sitting with the little ones on the school bench, peeped out, grimacing, from every letter of his grammar. Then when he was asleep the evil old man sat by his pillow . . . he drove away the bright spirits whose gold and sapphire wings rustled about his cot, carried off his poor mother from him for ever, and began whispering to him every night long, wonderful fairy tales, unintelligible to his childish imagination, but thrilling and tormenting him with terror and unchildlike passion. But the wicked old man did not heed his sobs and entreaties, and would go on talking to him till he sank into numbness, into unconsciousness. Then the child suddenly woke up a man; the years passed over him unseen, unheeded. He suddenly became aware of his real position. He understood all at once that he was alone, an alien to all the world, alone in a corner not his own, among mysterious and suspicious people, among enemies who were always gathering together and whispering in the corners of his dark room, and nodding to the old woman squatting on her heels near the fire, warming her bony old hands, and pointing to him. He sank into perplexity and uneasiness; he wanted to know who these people were, why they were here, why he was himself in this room, and guessed that he had strayed into some dark den of miscreants, drawn on by some powerful but incomprehensible force, without having first found out who and what the tenants were and who his landlord was. He began to be tortured by suspicion—and suddenly, in the stillness of the night, again there began a long, whispered story, and some old woman mournfully nodding her white, grizzled head before the dying fire, was muttering it softly, hardly audibly to herself. But—and again he was overcome with horror—the story took shape before him in forms and faces. He saw everything, from his dim, childish visions upwards: all his thoughts and dreams, all his experiences in life, all he had read in books, things he had forgotten long ago, all were coming to life, all were being put together, taking shape and rising up before him in colossal forms and images, moving and swarming about him; he saw spread out before him magnificent, enchanted gardens, a whole town built up and demolished before his eyes, a whole churchyard giving up its dead, who began living over again; whole races and peoples came into being and passed away before his eyes; finally, every one of his thoughts, every immaterial fancy, now took bodily shape around his sick-bed; took bodily shape almost at the moment of its conception: at last he saw himself thinking not in immaterial ideas, but in whole worlds, whole creations, saw himself borne along like an atom in this infinite, strange world from which there was no escape, and all this life in its mutinous independence crushing and oppressing him and pursuing him with eternal, infinite irony; he felt that he was dying, dissolving into dust and ashes for ever, and even without hope of resurrection; he tried to flee, but there was no corner in all the universe to hide him. At last, in an access of despair, he made an intense effort, uttered a shriek and woke up.

He woke up, bathed in a chill, icy sweat. About him was a deadly silence; it was the dead of night. But still it seemed to him that somewhere the wonderful fairy tale was going on, that some hoarse voice was really telling a long story of something that seemed familiar to him. He heard talk of dark forests, of bold brigands, of some daring bravoes, maybe of Stenka Razin himself, of merry drunken bargemen, of some fair maiden, and of Mother Volga. Was it not a fairy tale? Was he really hearing it? For a whole hour he lay, open-eyed, without stirring a muscle, in agonizing numbness. At last he got up carefully, and joyfully felt that his strength had come back to him after his severe illness. The delirium was over and reality was beginning. He noticed that he was dressed exactly as had been during his talk with Katerina, so that it could not have been long since the morning she had left him. The fire of resolution ran through his veins. Mechanically he felt with his hand for a big nail for some reason driven into the top of the partition near which stood his bed, seized it, and hanging his whole weight upon it, succeeded in pulling himself up to the crevice from which a hardly perceptible light stole into his room. He put his eye to the opening and, almost breathless with excitement, began peeping in.

There was a bed in the corner of the landlord's room; before it was a table covered with a cloth and piled up with books of old-fashioned shape, looking from their bindings like devotional books. In the corner was an ikon of the same old-fashioned pattern as in his room; a lamp was burning before it. On the bed lay the old man, Murin, sick, worn out with suffering and pale as a sheet, covered with a fur rug. On his knees was an open book. On a bench beside the bed lay Katerina, with her arm about the old man's chest and her head bent on his shoulder. She was looking at him with attentive, childishly wondering eyes, and seemed, breathless with expectation, to be listening with insatiable curiosity to what Murin was telling her. From time to time the speaker's voice rose higher, there was a shade of animation on his pale face; he frowned, his eyes began to flash, and Katerina seemed to turn pale with dread and expectation. Then something like a smile came into the old man's face and Katerina began laughing softly. Sometimes tears came into her eyes; then the old man tenderly stroked her on the head like a child, and she embraced him more tightly than ever with her bare arm that gleamed like snow, and nestled even more lovingly to his bosom.

At times Ordynov still thought this was part of his dream; in fact, he was convinced of it; but the blood rushed to his head and the veins throbbed painfully in his temples. He let go of the nail, got off the bed, and staggering, feeling his way like a lunatic, without understanding the impulse that flamed up like fire in his blood, he went to the door and pushed violently; the rusty bolt flew open at once, and with a bang and a crash he suddenly found himself in the middle of his landlord's bedroom. He saw Katerina start and tremble, saw the old man's eyes flash angrily under his lowering brows, and his whole face contorted with sudden fury. He saw the old man, still keeping close watch upon him, feel hurriedly with fumbling hand for a gun that hung upon the wall; then he saw the barrel of the gun flash, aimed straight at his breast with an uncertain hand that trembled with fury. . . . There was the sound of a shot, then a wild, almost unhuman, scream, and when the smoke parted, a terrible sight met Ordynov's eyes. Trembling all over, he bent over the old man. Murin was lying on the floor; he was writhing in convulsions, his face was contorted in agony and there was foam upon his working lips. Ordynov guessed that the unhappy man was in a severe epileptic fit. He flew, together with Katerina, to help him . . .

III

The whole night was spent in agitation. Next day Ordynov went out early in the morning, in spite of his weakness and the fever that still hung about him. In the yard he met the porter again. This time the Tatar lifted his cap to him from a distance and looked at him with curiosity. Then, as though pulling himself together, he set to work with his broom, glancing askance at Ordynov as the latter slowly approached him.

"Well, did you hear nothing in the night?" asked Ordynov

"Yes, I heard."

"What sort of man is he? Who is he?"

"Self took lodgings, self should know; me stranger."

"Will you ever speak?" cried Ordynov, beside himself with an access of morbid irritability.

"What did me do? Your fault—you frightened the tenants. Below lives the coffin-maker, he deaf, but heard it all, and his wife deaf, but she heard, and in next yard, far away, they heard, too. I go to the overseer."

"I am going to him myself," answered Ordynov; and he went to the gate.

"As you will; self took the room. . . . Master, master, stay."

Ordynov looked round; the porter touched his hat from politeness.

"Well!"

"If you go, I go to the landlord."

"What?"

"Better move."

"You're stupid," said Ordynov, and was going on again.

"Master, master, stay." The porter touched his hat again and grinned. "Listen, master: be not wrathful; why persecute a poor man? It's a sin to persecute a poor man. It is not God's law—do you hear?"

"You listen, too: here, take that. Come, what is he?"

"What is he?"

"Yes."

"I'll tell you without money."

At this point the porter took up his broom, brandished it once or twice, then stopped and looked intently, with an air of importance, at Ordynov.

"You're a nice gentleman. If you don't want to live with a good man, do as you like; that's what I say."

Then the Tatar looked at him still more expressively, and fell to sweeping furiously again.

Making a show of having finished something at last, he went up to Ordynov mysteriously, and with a very expressive gesture pronounced—

"This is how it is."

"How—what?"

"No sense."

"What?"

"Has flown away. Yes! Has flown away!" he repeated in a still more mysterious tone. "He is ill. He used to have a barge, a big one, and a second and a third, used to be on the Volga, and me from the Volga myself. He had a factory, too, but it was burnt down, and he is off his head."

"He is mad?"

"Nay! . . . Nay! . . ." the Tatar answered emphatically. "Not mad. He is a clever man. He knows everything; he has read many books, many, many; he has read everything, and tells others the truth. Some bring two roubles, three roubles, forty roubles, as much as you please; he looks in a book, sees and tells the whole truth. And the money's on the table at once—nothing without money!"

At this point the Tatar positively laughed with glee, throwing himself into Murin's interests with extreme zest.

"Why, does he tell fortunes, prophesy?"

"H'm! . . ." muttered the porter, wagging his head quickly. "He tells the truth. He prays, prays a great deal. It's just that way, comes upon him."

Then the Tatar made his expressive gesture again.

At that moment some one called the porter from the other yard, and then a little, bent, grey-headed man in a sheepskin appeared. He walked stumbling and looking at the ground, groaning and muttering to himself. He looked as though he were in his dotage.

"The master, the master!" the porter whispered in a fluster, with a hurried nod to Ordynov, and taking off his cap, he ran to meet the old man, whose face looked familiar to Ordynov; he had anyway met him somewhere just lately.

Reflecting, however, that there was nothing remarkable in that, he walked out of the yard. The porter struck him as an out-and-out rogue and an impudent fellow.

"The scoundrel was practically bargaining with me!" he thought. "Goodness knows what it means!"

He had reached the street as he said this.

By degrees he began to be absorbed in other thoughts. The impression was unpleasant, the day was grey and cold; flakes of snow were flying. The young man felt overcome by a feverish shiver again; he felt, too, as though the earth were shaking under him. All at once an unpleasantly sweet, familiar voice wished him good-morning in a broken tenor.

"Yaroslav Ilyitch," said Ordynov.

Before him stood a short, sturdy, red-checked man, apparently about thirty, with oily grey eyes and a little smile, dressed . . . as Yaroslav Ilyitch always was dressed. He was holding out his hand to him in a very amicable way. Ordynov had made the acquaintance of Yaroslav Ilyitch just a year before in quite a casual way, almost in the street. They had so easily become acquainted, partly by chance and partly through Yaroslav Ilyitch's extraordinary propensity for picking up everywhere good-natured, well-bred people, and his preference for friends of good education whose talents and elegance of behaviour made them worthy at least of belonging to good society. Though Yaroslav Ilyitch had an extremely sweet tenor, yet even in conversation with his dearest friends there was something extraordinarily clear, powerful and dominating in the tone of his voice that would put up with no evasions; it was perhaps merely due to habit.

"How on earth . . . ?" exclaimed Yaroslav Ilyitch, with an expression of the most genuine, ecstatic pleasure.

"I am living here."

"Have you lived here long?" Yaroslav Ilyitch continued on an ascending note. "And I did not know it! Why, we are neighbours! I am in this quarter now, I came back from the Ryazan province a month ago. I've caught you, my old and noble friend!" and Yaroslav Ilyitch laughed in a most good-natured way. "Sergeyev!" he cried impressively, "wait for me at Tarasov's, and don't let them touch a sack without me. And stir up the Olsufyev porter: tell him to come to the office at once. I shall be there in an hour. . . . "

Hurriedly giving some one this order, the refined Yaroslav Ilyitch took Ordynov's arm and led him to the nearest restaurant.

"I shall not be satisfied till we have had a couple of words alone after such a long separation. Well, what of your doings?" he pronounced almost reverently, dropping his voice mysteriously. "Working at science, as ever?"

"Yes, as before," answered Ordynov, struck by a bright idea.

"Splendid, Vassily Mihalitch, splendid!" At this point Yaroslav Ilyitch pressed Ordynov's hand warmly. "You will be a credit to the community. God give you luck in your career. . . . Goodness! how glad I am I met you! How often I have thought of you, how often I have said: 'Where is he, our good, noble-hearted, witty Vassily Mihalitch?'"

They engaged a private room. Yaroslav Ilyitch ordered lunch, asked for vodka, and looked feelingly at Ordynov.

"I have read a great deal since I saw you," he began in a timid and somewhat insinuating voice. "I have read all Pushkin . . ."

Ordynov looked at him absent-mindedly.

"A marvellous understanding of human passion. But first of all, let me express my gratitude. You have done so much for me by nobly instilling into me a right way of thinking."

"Upon my word . . ."

"No, let me speak; I always like to pay honour where honour is due, and I am proud that this feeling at least has found expression."

"Really, you are unfair to yourself, and I, indeed . . ."

"No, I am quite fair," Yaroslav Ilyitch replied, with extraordinary warmth. "What am I in comparison with you?"

"Good Heavens!"

"Yes. . . ."

Then followed silence.

"Following your advice, I have dropped many low acquaintances and have, to some extent, softened the coarseness of my manners," Yaroslav Ilyitch began again in a somewhat timid and insinuating voice. "In the time when I am free from my duties I sit for the most part at home; in the evenings I read some improving book and . . . I have only one desire, Vassily Mihalitch: to be of some little use to the fatherland. . . . "

"I have always thought you a very high-minded man, Yaroslav Ilyitch."

"You always bring balm to my spirit . . . you generous young man. . . ."

Yaroslav Ilyitch pressed Ordynov's hand warmly.

"You are drinking nothing?" he said, his enthusiasm subsiding a little.

"I can't; I'm ill."

"Ill? Yes, are you really? How long—in what way—did you come to be ill? If you like I'll speak . . . What doctor is treating you? If you like I'll speak to our parish doctor. I'll run round to him myself. He's a very skilful man!"

Yaroslav Ilyitch was already picking up his hat.

"Thank you very much. I don't go in for being doctored. I don't like doctors."

"You don't say so? One can't go on like that. But he's a very clever man," Yaroslav Ilyitch went on imploringly. "The other day—do allow me to tell you this, dear Vassily Mihalitch—the other day a poor carpenter came. 'Here,' said he, 'I hurt my hand with a tool; cure it for me. . . .' Semyon Pafnutyitch, seeing that the poor fellow was in danger of gangrene, set to work to cut off the wounded hand; he did this in my presence, but it was done in such a gener . . . that is, in such a superb way, that I confess if it had not been for compassion for suffering humanity, it would have been a pleasure to look on, simply from curiosity. But where and how did you fall ill?"

"In moving from my lodging . . . I've only just got up."

"But you are still very unwell and you ought not to be out. So you are not living where you were before? But what induced you to move?"

"My landlady was leaving Petersburg."

"Domna Savishna? Really? . . . A thoroughly estimable, good-hearted woman! Do you know? I had almost a son's respect for her. That life, so near its end, had something of the serene dignity of our forefathers, and looking at her, one seemed to see the incarnation of our hoary-headed, stately old traditions . . . I mean of that . . . something in it so poetical!' Yaroslav Ilyitch concluded, completely overcome with shyness and blushing to his ears.

"Yes, she was a nice woman."

"But allow me to ask you where you are settled now."

"Not far from here, in Koshmarov's Buildings."

"I know him. A grand old man! I am, I may say, almost a real friend of his. A fine old veteran!"

Yaroslav Ilyitch's lips almost quivered with enthusiasm. He asked for another glass of vodka and a pipe.

"Have you taken a flat?"

"No, a furnished room in a flat."

"Who is your landlord? Perhaps I know him, too."

"Murin, an artisan; a tall old man . . ."

"Murin, Murin; yes, in the back court, over the coffin-maker's, allow me to ask?"

"Yes, yes, in the back court."

"H'm! are you comfortable there?"

"Yes; I've only just moved in."

"H'm! . . . I only meant to say, h'm! . . . have you noticed nothing special?"

"Really . . ."

"That is . . . I am sure you will be all right there if you are satisfied with your quarters. . . . I did not mean that; I am ready to warn you . . . but, knowing your character . . . How did that old artisan strike you?"

"He seems to be quite an invalid."

"Yes, he's a great sufferer. . . . But have you noticed nothing? Have you talked to him?"

"Very little; he is so morose and unsociable."

"H'm! . . ." Yaroslav Ilyitch mused. "He's an unfortunate man," he said dreamily.

"Is he?"

"Yes, unfortunate, and at the same time an incredibly strange and interesting person. However, if he does not worry you . . . Excuse my dwelling upon such a subject, but I was curious . . ."

"And you have really roused my curiosity, too. . . . I should very much like to know what sort of a man he is. Besides, I am living with him. . . ."

"You know, they say the man was once very rich. He traded, as most likely you have heard. But through various unfortunate circumstances he was reduced to poverty; many of his barges were wrecked in a storm and lost, together with their cargo. His factory, which was, I believe, in the charge of a near and dear relation, was equally unlucky and was burnt down, and the relation himself perished in the flames. It must be admitted it was a terrible loss! Then, so they say, Murin sank into tearful despondency; they began to be afraid he would lose his reason, and, indeed, in a quarrel with another merchant, also an owner of barges plying on the Volga, he suddenly showed himself in such a strange and unexpected fight that the whole incident could only be accounted for on the supposition that he was quite mad, which I am prepared to believe. I have heard in detail of some of his queer ways; there suddenly happened at last a very strange, so to say momentous, circumstance which can only be attributed to the malign influence of wrathful destiny."

"What was it?" asked Ordynov.

"They say that in a fit of madness he made an attempt on the life of a young merchant, of whom he had before been very fond. He was so upset when he recovered from the attack that he was on the point of taking his own life; so at least they say. I don't know what happened after that, but it is known that he was several years doing penance. . . . But what is the matter with you, Vassily Mihalitch? Am I fatiguing you with my artless tale?"

"Oh no, for goodness' sake . . . You say that he has been doing penance; but he is not alone."

"I don't know. I am told he was alone. Anyway, no one else was mixed up in that affair. However, I have not heard what followed; I only know . . ."

"Well?"

"I only know—that is, I had nothing special in my mind to add . . . I only want to say, if you find anything strange or out of the ordinary in him, all that is merely the result of the misfortunes that have descended upon him one after the other. . . ."

"Yes, he is so devout, so sanctimonious."

"I don't think so, Vassily Mihalitch; he has suffered so much; I believe he is quite sincere."

"But now, of course, he is not mad; he is all right."

"Oh, yes, yes; I can answer for that, I am ready to take my oath on it; he is in full possession of all his faculties. He is only, as you have justly observed, extremely strange and devout. He is a very sensible man, in fact. He speaks smartly, boldly and very subtly. The traces of his stormy life in the past are still visible on his face. He's a curious man, and very well read.

"He seems to be always reading religious books."

"Yes, he is a mystic."

"What?"

"A mystic. But I tell you that as a secret. I will tell you, as a secret, too, that a very careful watch was kept on him for a time. The man had a great influence on people who used to go to him."

"What sort of influence?"

"But you'll never believe it; you see, in those days he did not live in this building; Alexandr Ignatyevitch, a respectable citizen, a man of standing, held in universal esteem, went to see him with a lieutenant out of curiosity. They arrive and are received, and the strange man begins by looking into their faces. He usually looks into people's faces if he consents to be of use to them; if not, he sends people away, and even very uncivilly, I'm told. He asks them, 'What do you want, gentlemen?' 'Well,' answers Alexandr Ignatyevitch, 'your gift can tell you that, without our saying.' 'Come with me into the next room,' he says; then he signified which of them it was who needed his services. Alexandr Ignatyevitch did not say what happened to him afterwards, but he came out from him as white as a sheet. The same thing happened to a well-known lady of high rank: she, too, came out from seeing him as white as a sheet, bathed in tears and overcome with his predictions and his sayings."

"Strange. But now does he still do the same?"

"It's strictly prohibited. There have been marvellous instances. A young cornet, the hope and joy of a distinguished family, mocked at him. 'What are you laughing at?' said the old man, angered. 'In three days' time you will be like this!' and he crossed his arms over his bosom to signify a corpse."

"Well?"

"I don't venture to believe it, but they say his prediction came true. He has a gift, Vassily Mihalitch. . . . You are pleased to smile at my guileless story. I know that you are greatly ahead of me in culture; but I believe in him; he's not a charlatan. Pushkin himself mentions a similar case in his works."

"H'm! I don't want to contradict you. I think you said he's not living alone?"

"I don't know . . . I believe his daughter is with him."

"Daughter?"

"Yes, or perhaps his wife; I know there is some woman with him. I have had a passing glimpse of her, but I did not notice."

"H'm! Strange . . ."

The young man fell to musing, Yaroslav Ilyitch to tender contemplation of him. He was touched both at seeing an old friend and at having satisfactorily told him something very interesting. He sat sucking his pipe with his eyes fixed on Vassily Mihalitch; but suddenly he jumped up in a fluster.

A whole hour has passed and I forgot the time! Dear Vassily Mihalitch, once more I thank the lucky chance that brought us together, but it is time for me to be off. Will you allow me to visit you in your learned retreat?"

Please do, I shall be delighted. I will come and see you, too, when I have a chance."

"That's almost too pleasant to believe. You gratify me, you gratify me unutterably! You would not believe how you have delighted me!"

They went out of the restaurant, Sergeyev was already flying to meet them and to report in a hurried sentence that Vilyam Emelyanovitch was pleased to be driving out. A pair of spirited roans in a smart light gig did, in fact, come into sight. The trace horse was particularly fine. Yaroslav Ilyitch pressed his best friend's hand as though in a vice, touched his hat and set off to meet the flying gig. On the way he turned round once or twice to nod farewells to Ordynov.

Ordynov felt so tired, so exhausted in every limb, that he could scarcely move his legs. He managed somehow to crawl home. At the gate he was met again by the porter, who had been diligently watching his parting from Yaroslav Ilyitch, and beckoning to him from a distance. But the young man passed him by. At the door of his flat he ran full tilt against a little grey-headed figure coming out from Murin's room, looking on the ground.

"Lord forgive my transgressions!" whispered the figure, skipping on one side with the springiness of a cork.

"Did I hurt you?"

"No, I humbly thank you for your civility. . . . Oh, Lord, Lord!"

The meek little man, groaning and moaning and muttering something edifying to himself, went cautiously down the stairs. This was the "master" of the house, of whom the porter stood in such awe. Only then Ordynov remembered that he had seen him for the first time, here at Murin's, when he was moving into the lodging.

He felt unhinged and shaken; he knew that his imagination and impressionability were strained to the utmost pitch, and resolved not to trust himself. By degrees he sank into a sort of apathy. A heavy oppressive feeling weighed upon his chest. His heart ached as though it were sore all over, and his whole soul was full of dumb, comfortless tears.

He fell again upon the bed which she had made him, and began listening again. He heard two breathings: one the heavy broken breathing of a sick man, the other soft but uneven, as though also stirred by emotion, as though that heart was beating with the same yearning, with the same passion. At times he heard the rustle of her dress, the faint stir of her soft steps, and even that faint stir of her feet echoed with the vague but agonizingly sweet pang in his heart. At last he seemed to distinguish sobs, rebellious sighs, and at last, praying again. He knew that she was kneeling before the ikon, wringing her hands in a frenzy of despair! . . . Who was she? For whom was she praying? By what desperate passion was her heart torn? Why did it ache and grieve and pour itself out in such hot and hopeless tears?

He began to recall her words. All that she had said to him was still ringing in his ears like music, and his heart lovingly responded with a vague heavy throb at every recollection, every word of hers as he devoutly repeated it. . . . For an instant a thought flashed through his mind that he had dreamed all this. But at the same moment his whole being ached in swooning anguish as the impression of her hot breath, her words, her kiss rose vividly again in his imagination. He closed his eyes and sank into oblivion. A clock struck somewhere; it was getting late; twilight was falling.

It suddenly seemed to him that she was bending over him again, that she was looking into his eyes with her exquisitely clear eyes, wet with sparkling tears of serene, happy joy, soft and bright as the infinite turquoise vault of heaven at hot midday. Her face beamed with such triumphant peace; her smile was warm with such solemnity of infinite bliss; she leaned with such sympathy, with such childlike impulsiveness on his shoulder that a moan of joy broke from his exhausted bosom. She tried to tell him something, caressingly she confided something to him. Again it was as though heartrending music smote upon his hearing. Greedily he drank in the air, warm, electrified by her near breathing. In anguish he stretched out his arms, sighed, opened his eyes. . . . She stood before him, bending down to his face, all pale as from fear, all in tears, all quivering with emotion. She was saying something to him, entreating him with half-bare arms, clasping and wringing her hands; he folded her in his arms, she quivered on his bosom . . .

PART II

I

"What is it? What is the matter with you?" said Ordynov, waking up completely, still pressing her in his strong, warm embrace. "What is the matter with you, Katerina? What is it, my love?"

She sobbed softly with downcast eyes, hiding her flushed face on his breast. For a long while she could not speak and kept trembling as though in terror.

"I don't know, I don't know," she said at last, in a hardly audible voice, gasping for breath, and scarcely able to articulate. "I don't know how I came here . . ." She clasped him even more tightly, with even more intensity, and in a violent irrepressible rush of feeling, kissed his shoulder, his hands, his chest; at last, as though in despair, she hid her face in her hands, fell on her knees, and buried her head in his knees. When Ordynov, in inexpressible anguish, lifted her up impatiently and made her sit down beside him, her whole face glowed with a full flush of shame, her weeping eyes sought forgiveness, and the smile that, in spite of herself, played on her lip could scarcely subdue the violence of her new feeling. Now she seemed again frightened, mistrustfully she pushed away his hand, and, with drooping head, answered his hurried questions in a fearful whisper.

"Perhaps you have had a terrible dream?" said Ordynov. "Perhaps you have seen some vision . . . Yes? Perhaps *he* has frightened you. . . . He is delirious and unconscious. Perhaps he has said something that was not for you to hear? Did you hear something? Yes?"

"No, I have not been asleep," answered Katerina, stifling her emotion with an effort. "Sleep did not come to

me, he has been silent all the while and only once he called
me. I went up, called his name, spoke to him; I was
frightened; he did not wake and did not hear me. He is
terribly sick, the Lord succour him! Then misery came
upon my heart, bitter misery! I prayed and prayed and then
this came upon me."

"Hush, Katerina, hush, my life, hush! You were
frightened yesterday. . . ."

"No, I was not frightened yesterday! . . ."

"Has it ever been like this with you at other times?"

"Yes." And again she trembled all over and huddled up
to him like a child. "You see," she said, repressing her sobs,
"it was not for nothing that I have come to you, it was not
for nothing that I could not bear to stay alone," she
repeated, gratefully pressing his hands. "Enough, enough
shedding tears over other people's sorrows! Save them for a
dark day when you are lonely and cast down and there is no
one with you! . . . Listen, have you ever had a love?"

"No. . . . I never knew a love before you. . . ."

"Before me? . . . You call me your love?"

She suddenly looked at him as though surprised, would
have said something, but then was silent and looked down.
By degrees her whole face suddenly flushed again a
glowing crimson; her eyes shone more brightly through the
forgotten tears still warm on her eyelashes, and it could be
seen that some question was hovering on her lips. With
bashful shyness she looked at him once or twice and then
looked down again.

"No, it is not for me to be your first love," she said.
"No, no," she said, shaking her head thoughtfully, while the
smile stole gently again over her face. "No," she said, at
last, laughing; "it's not for me, my own, to be your love."

At that point she glanced at him, but there was suddenly
such sadness reflected in her face, such hopeless sorrow
suddenly overshadowed all her features, such despair all at

once surged up from within, from her heart, that Ordynov was overwhelmed by an unaccountable, painful feeling of compassion for her mysterious grief and looked at her with indescribable distress.

"Listen to what I say to you," she said in a voice that wrung his heart, pressing his hands in hers, struggling to stifle her sobs. "Heed me well, listen, my joy! You calm your heart and do not love me as you love me now. It will be better for you, your heart will be lighter and gladder, and you will guard yourself from a fell foe and will win a sister fond. I will come and see you as you please, fondle you and take no shame upon myself for making friends with you. I was with you for two days when you lay in that cruel sickness! Get to know your sister! It is not for nothing that we have sworn to be brother and sister, it is not for nothing that I prayed and wept to the Holy Mother for you! You won't get another sister! You may go all round the world, you may get to knew the whole earth and not find another love like mine, if it is love your heart wants. I will love you warmly, I will always love you as I do now, and I will love you because your soul is pure and clean and can be seen through; because when first I glanced at you, at once I knew you were the guest of my house, the longed-for guest, and it was not for nothing that you wanted to come to us; I love you because when you look at me your eyes are full of love and speak for your heart, and when they say anything, at once I know of all that is within you and long to give my life for your love, my freedom, because it is sweet to be even a slave to the man whose heart I have found. . . . But my life is not mine but another's . . . and my freedom is bound! Take me for a sister and be a brother to me and take me to your heart when misery, when cruel weakness falls upon me; only do so that I have no shame to come to you and sit through the long night with you as now. Do you hear me? Is your heart opened to me? Do you understand what I have been saying to you? . ."

She tried to say something more, glanced at him, laid her hand on his shoulder and at last sank helpless on his bosom. Her voice died away in convulsive, passionate sobbing, her bosom heaved and her face flushed like an evening sunset.

"My life," whispered Ordynov; everything was dark before his eyes and he could hardly breathe. "My joy," he said, not knowing what he was saying, not understanding himself, trembling lest a breath should break the spell, should destroy everything that was happening, which he took rather for a vision than reality: so misty was everything around him! "I don't know, I don't understand you, I don't remember what you have just said to me, my mind is darkened, my heart aches, my queen!"

At this point his voice broke with emotion. She clung more tightly, more warmly, more fervently to him. He got up, no longer able to restrain himself; shattered, exhausted by ecstasy, he fell on his knees. Convulsive sobs broke agonizingly from his breast at last, and the voice that came straight from his heart quivered like a harp-string, from the fulness of unfathomable ecstasy and bliss.

"Who are you, who are you, my own? Where do you come from, my darling?" he said, trying to stifle his sobs. "From what heaven did you fly into my sphere? It's like a dream about me, I cannot believe in you. Don't check me, let me speak, let me tell you all, all! I have long wanted to speak . . . Who are you, who are you, my joy? How did you find my heart? Tell me; have you long been my sister? . . . Tell me everything about yourself, where you have been till now. Tell me what the place was called where you lived; what did you love there at first? what rejoiced you? what grieved you? . . . Was the air warm? was the sky clear? . . . Who were dear to you? who loved you before me? to whom did your soul yearn first? . . . Had you a mother? did she pet you as a child, or did you look round upon life as solitary as I did? Tell me, were you always like this? What were your dreams? what were your visions of the future? what was fulfilled and what was unfulfilled with you?—tell me everything. . . . For whom did your maiden heart yearn first, and for what did you give it? Tell me, what must I give you for it? what must I give you for yourself? . . . Tell me, my darling, my light, my sister; tell me, how am I to win your heart? . . ."

Then his voice broke again, and he bowed his head. But when he raised his eyes, dumb horror froze his heart and the hair stood up on his head.

Katerina was sitting pale as a sheet. She was looking with a fixed stare into the air, her lips were blue as a corpse's and her eyes were dimmed by a mute, agonizing woe. She stood up slowly, took two steps forward and, with a piercing wail, flung herself down before the ikon. . . . Jerky, incoherent words broke from her throat. She lost consciousness. Shaken with horror Ordynov lifted her up and carried her to his bed; he stood over her, frantic. A minute later she opened her eyes, sat up in the bed, looked about her and seized his hand. She drew him towards her, tried to whisper something with her lips that were still pale, but her voice would not obey her. At last she burst into a flood of tears; the hot drops scalded Ordynov's chilly hand.

"It's hard for me, it's hard for me now; my last hour is at hand!" she said at last in desperate anguish.

She tried to say something else, but her faltering tongue could not utter a word. She looked in despair at Ordynov, who did not understand her. He bent closer to her and listened. . . . At last he heard her whisper distinctly—

"I am corrupted—they have corrupted me, they have ruined me!"

Ordynov lifted his head and looked at her in wild amazement. Some hideous thought flashed across his mind. Katerina saw the convulsive workings of his face.

"Yes! Corrupted," she went on; "a wicked man corrupted me. It is *he* who has ruined me! . . . I have sold my soul to him. Why, why did you speak of my mother? Why did you want to torture me? God, God be your judge! . . ."

A minute later she was softly weeping; Ordynov's heart was beating and aching in mortal anguish.

"He says," she whispered in a restrained, mysterious voice, "that when he dies he will come and fetch my sinful soul. . . . I am his, I have sold my soul to him. He tortures me, he reads to me in his books. Here, look at his book! here is his book. He says I have committed the unpardonable sin. Look, look . . ."

And she showed him a book. Ordynov did not notice where it had come from. He took it mechanically—it was all in manuscript like the old heretical books which he had happened to see before, but now he was incapable of looking or concentrating his attention on anything else. The book fell out of his hands. He softly embraced Katerina, trying to bring her to reason. "Hush hush," he said; "they have frightened you. I am with you; rest with me, my own, my love, my light."

"You know nothing, nothing," she said, warmly pressing his hand. "I am always like this! I am always afraid. . . . I've tortured you enough, enough! . . ."

"I go to him then," she began a minute later, taking a breath; "sometimes he simply comforts me with his words, sometimes he takes his book, the biggest, and reads it over me—he always reads such grim, threatening things! I don't know what, and don't understand every word; but fear comes upon me; and when I listen to his voice, it is as though it were not he speaking, but some one else, some one evil, some one you could not soften anyhow, could not entreat, and one's heart grows so heavy and burns. . . . Heavier than when this misery comes upon me!"

"Don't go to him. Why do you go to him?" said Ordynov, hardly conscious of his own words.

"Why have I come to you? If you ask—I don't know either. . . . But he keeps saying to me, 'Pray, pray!' Sometimes I get up in the dark night and for a long time, for hours together, I pray; sometimes sleep overtakes me, but fear always wakes me, always wakes me and then I always fancy that a storm is gathering round me, that harm is coming to me, that evil things will tear me to pieces and torment me, that my prayers will not reach the saints, and that they will not save me from cruel grief. My soul is being torn, my whole body seems breaking to pieces through crying. . . . Then I begin praying again, and pray and pray until the Holy Mother looks down on me from the ikon, more lovingly. Then I get up and go away to sleep, utterly shattered; sometimes I wake up on the floor, on my knees before the ikon. Then sometimes he wakes, calls me, begins to soothe me, caress me, comfort me, and then I feel better, and if any trouble comes I am not afraid with him. He is powerful! His word is mighty!"

"But what trouble, what sort of trouble have you?" . . . And Ordynov wrung his hands in despair.

Katerina turned fearfully pale. She looked at him like one condemned to death, without hope of pardon.

"Me? I am under a curse, I'm a murderess; my mother cursed me! I was the ruin of my own mother! . . ."

Ordynov embraced her without a word. She nestled tremulously to him. He felt a convulsive shiver pass all over her, and it seemed as though her soul were parting from her body.

"I hid her in the damp earth," she said, overwhelmed by the horror of her recollections, and lost in visions of her irrevocable past. "I have long wanted to tell it; he always forbade me with supplications, upbraidings, and angry words, and at times he himself will arouse all my anguish as though he were my enemy and adversary. At night, even as now—it all comes into my mind. Listen, listen! It was long ago, very long ago, I don't remember when, but it is all before me as though it had been yesterday, like a dream of yesterday, devouring my heart all night. Misery makes the time twice as long. Sit here, sit here beside me; I will tell you all my sorrow; may I be struck down, accursed as I am, by a mother's curse. . . . I am putting my life into your hands . . ."

Ordynov tried to stop her, but she folded her hands, beseeching his love to attend, and then, with even greater agitation began to speak. Her story was incoherent, the turmoil of her spirit could be felt in her words, but Ordynov understood it all, because her life had become his life, her grief his grief, and because her foe stood visible before him, taking shape and growing up before him with every word she uttered and, as it were, with inexhaustible strength crushing his heart and cursing him malignantly. His blood was in a turmoil, it flooded his heart and obscured his reason. The wicked old man of his dream (Ordynov believed this) was living before him.

"Well, it was a night like this," Katerina began, "only stormier, and the wind in our forest howled as I had never heard it before . . . it was in that night that my ruin began! An oak was broken before our window, and an old grey-headed beggar came to our door, and he said that he remembered that oak as a little child, and that it was the same then as when the wind blew it down. . . . That night—as I remember now—my father's barge was wrecked on the river by a storm, and though he was afflicted with illness, he drove to the place as soon as the fishermen ran to us at the factory. Mother and I were sitting alone. I was asleep.

She was sad about something and weeping bitterly . . . and I knew what about! She had just been ill, she was still pale and kept telling me to get ready her shroud. . . . Suddenly, at midnight, we heard a knock at the gate; I jumped up, the blood rushed to my heart; mother cried out. . . . I did not look at her, I was afraid. I took a lantern and went myself to open the gate. . . . It was *he*! I felt frightened, because I was always frightened when he came, and it was so with me from childhood ever since I remembered anything! At that time he had not white hair; his beard was black as pitch, his eyes burnt like coals; until that time he had never once looked at me kindly. He asked me, 'Is your mother at home?' Shutting the little gate, I answered that 'Father was not at home.' He said, 'I know,' and suddenly looked at me, looked at me in such a way . . . it was the first time he had looked at me like that. I went on, but he still stood. 'Why don't you come in?' 'I am thinking.' By then we were going up to the room. 'Why did you say that father was not at home when I asked you whether mother was at home?' I said nothing. . . . Mother was terror-stricken—she rushed to him. . . . He scarcely glanced at her. I saw it all. He was all wet and shivering; the storm had driven him fifteen miles, but whence he came and where he lived neither mother nor I ever knew; we had not seen him for nine weeks. . . . He threw down his cap, pulled off his gloves—did not pray to the ikon, nor bow to his hostess—he sat down by the fire . . ."

Katerina passed her hand over her face, as though something were weighing upon her and oppressing her, but a minute later she raised her head and began again—

"He began talking in Tatar to mother. Mother knew it, I don't understand a word. Other times when he came, they sent me away; but this time mother dared not say a word to her own child. The unclean spirit gained possession of my soul and I looked at my mother, exalting myself in my heart. I saw they were looking at me, they were talking about me; she began crying. I saw him clutch at his knife and more than once of late I had seen him clutch at the knife when he was talking with mother. I jumped up and caught at his belt, tried to tear the evil knife away from him. He clenched his teeth, cried out and tried to beat me back; he struck me in the breast but did not shake me off. I thought I should die on the spot, there was a mist before my eyes. I fell on the floor, but did not cry out. Though I could hardly see, I saw him. He took off his belt, tucked up his sleeve, with the hand with which he had struck me took out the knife and gave it to me. 'Here, cut it away, amuse yourself over it, even as I insulted you, while I, proud girl, will bow down to the earth to you for it.' I laid aside the knife; the blood began to stifle me, I did not look at him. I remember I laughed without opening my lips and looked threateningly straight into mother's mournful eyes, and the shameless laugh never left my lips, while mother sat pale, deathlike . . ." With strained attention Ordynov listened to her incoherent story. By degrees her agitation subsided after the first outburst; her words grew calmer. The poor creature was completely carried away by her memories and her misery was spread over their limitless expanse.

"He took his cap without bowing. I took the lantern again to see him out instead of mother who, though she was ill, would have followed him. We reached the gates. I opened the little gate to him, drove away the dogs in silence. I see him take off his cap and bow to me, I see him feel in his bosom, take out a red morocco box, open the catch. I look in—big pearls, an offering to me. 'I have a beauty,' says he, 'in the town. I got it to offer to her, but I did not take it to her; take it, fair maiden, cherish your beauty; take them, though you crush them under foot.' I took them, but I did not want to stamp on them, I did not want to do them too much honour, but I took them like a viper, not saying a word. I came in and set them on the table before mother—it was for that I took them. Mother was silent for a minute, all white as a handkerchief. She speaks to me as though she fears me. 'What is this, Katya?' and I answer, 'The merchant brought them for you, my own—I know nothing.' I see the tears stream from her eyes. I see her gasp for breath. 'Not for me, Katya, not for me, wicked daughter, not for me.' I remember she said it so bitterly, so bitterly, as though she were weeping out her whole soul. I raised my eyes, I wanted to throw myself at her feet, but suddenly the evil one prompted me. 'Well, if not to you, most likely to father; I will give them to him when he comes back; I will say the merchants have been, they have forgotten their wares . . .' Then how she wept, my own. . . . 'I will tell him myself what merchants have been, and for what wares they came. . . . I will tell him whose daughter you are, whose bastard child! You are not my daughter now, you serpent's fry! You are my accursed child!' I say nothing, tears do not come to me. . . .I went up to my room and all night I listened to the storm, while I fitted my thoughts to its raging.

"Meanwhile, five days passed by. Towards evening after five days, father came in, surly and menacing, and he had been stricken by illness on the way. I saw his arm was bound up, I guessed that his enemy had waylaid him upon the road, his enemy had worn him out and brought sickness upon him. I knew, too, who was his enemy, I knew it all. He did not say a word to mother, he did not ask about me. He called together all the workmen, made them leave the factory, and guard the house from the evil eye. I felt in my heart, in that hour, that all was not well with the house. We waited, the night came, another stormy, snowy one, and dread came over my soul. I opened the window; my face was hot, my eyes were weeping, my restless heart was burning; I was on fire. I longed to be away from that room, far away to the land of light, where the thunder and lightning are born. My maiden heart was beating and beating. . . . Suddenly, in the dead of night, I was dozing, or a mist had fallen over my soul, and confounded it all of a sudden—I hear a knock at the window: 'Open!' I look, there was a man at the window, he had climbed up by a rope. I knew at once who the visitor was, I opened the window and let him into my lonely room. It was *he*! Without taking off his hat, he sat down on the bench, he panted and drew his breath as though he had been pursued. I stood in the corner and knew myself that I turned white all over. 'Is your father at home?' 'He is.' 'And your mother?' 'Mother is at home, too.' 'Be silent now; do you hear?' 'I hear.' 'What?' 'A whistle under the window!' 'Well, fair maid, do you want to cut your foe's head off? Call your father, take my life? I am at your maiden mercy; here is the cord, tie it, if your heart bids you; avenge yourself for your insult.' I am silent. 'Well? Speak, my joy.' 'What do you want?' 'I want my enemy to be gone, to take leave for good and all of the old love, and to lay my heart at the feet of a new one, a fair maid like you. . . .' I laughed; and I don't know how his evil words went to my heart. 'Let me, fair maid, walk downstairs, test my courage, pay homage to my hosts.' I trembled all over, my teeth knocked together, but my heart was like a red-hot iron. I went. I opened the door to him, I let him into the house, only on the threshold with an effort I brought out, 'Here, take your pearls and never give me a gift again,' and I threw the box after him."

Here Katerina stopped to take breath. At one moment she was pale and trembling like a leaf, at the next the blood rushed to her head, and now, when she stopped, her cheeks glowed with fire, her eyes flashed through her tears, and her bosom heaved with her laboured, uneven breathing. But suddenly she turned pale again and her voice sank with a mournful and tremulous quiver.

"Then I was left alone and the storm seemed to wrap me about. All at once I hear a shout, I hear workmen run across the yard to the factory, I hear them say, 'The factory is on fire.' I kept in hiding; all ran out of the house; I was left with mother; I knew that she was parting from life, that she had been lying for the last three days on her death-bed. I knew it, accursed daughter! . . . All at once a cry under my room, a faint cry like a child when it is frightened in its sleep, and then all was silent. I blew out the candle, I was as chill as ice, I hid my face in my hands, I was afraid to look. Suddenly I hear a shout close by, I hear the men running from the factory. I hung out of the window, I see them bearing my dead father, I hear them saying among themselves, 'He stumbled, he fell down the stairs into a red-hot cauldron; so the devil must have pushed him down.' I fell upon my bed; I waited, all numb with terror, and I do not know for whom or what I waited, only I was overwhelmed with woe in that hour. I don't remember how long I waited; I remember that suddenly everything began rocking, my head grew heavy, my eyes were smarting with smoke and I was glad that my end was near. Suddenly I felt some one lift me by the shoulders. I looked as best I could; he was singed all over and his kaftan, hot to the touch, was smoking."

"'I've come for you, fair maid; lead me away from trouble as before you led me into trouble; I have lost my soul for your sake, no prayers of mine can undo this accursed night! Maybe we will pray together!' He laughed, the wicked man. 'Show me,' said he, 'how to get out without passing people!' I took his hand and led him after me. We went through the corridor—the keys were with me—I opened the door to the store-room and pointed to the window. The window looked into the garden, he seized me in his powerful arms, embraced me and leapt with me out of the window. We ran together, hand-in-hand, we ran together for a long time. We looked, we were in a thick, dark forest. He began listening: 'There's a chase after us, Katya! There's a chase after us, fair maid, but it is not for us in this hour to lay down our lives! Kiss me, fair maid, for love and ever-lasting happiness!' 'Why are your hands covered with blood?' 'My hands covered with blood, my own? I stabbed your dogs; they barked too loud at a late guest. Come along!'"

"We ran on again; we saw in the path my father's horse, he had broken his bridle and run out of the stable; so he did not want to be burnt. 'Get on it, Katya, with me; God has sent us help.' I was silent. 'Won't you? I am not a heathen, not an unclean pagan; here, I will cross myself if you like,' and here he made the sign of the cross. I got on the horse, huddled up to him and forgot everything on his bosom, as though a dream had come over me, and when I woke I saw that we were standing by a broad, broad river. He got off the horse, lifted me down and went off to the reeds where his boat was hidden. We were getting in. 'Well, farewell, good horse; go to a new master, the old masters all forsake you!' I ran to father's horse and embraced him warmly at parting. Then we got in, he took the oars and in an instant we lost sight of the shore. And when could not see the shore, I saw him lay down the oars and look about him, all over the water."

"'Hail,' he said, 'stormy river-mother, who giveth to God's people and food to me! Say, hast thou guarded my goods, are my wares safe, while I've been away?' I sat mute, I cast down my eyes to my bosom; my face burned with shame as with a flame. And he: 'Thou art welcome to take all, stormy and insatiable river, only let me keep my vow and cherish my priceless pearl! Drop but one word, fair maid, send a ray of sunshine into the storm, scatter the dark night with light!'"

"He laughed as he spoke, his heart was burning for me, but I could not bear his jeers for shame; I longed to say a word, but was afraid and sat dumb. 'Well, then, be it so!' he answer to my timid thought; he spoke as though in sorrow, as though grief had come upon him, too. 'So one can take nothing by force. God be with you, you proud one, my dove, my fair maid! It seems, strong is your hatred for me, or I do not find favour in your clear eyes!' I listened and was seized by spite, seized by spite and love; I steeled my heart. I said: 'Pleasing or not pleasing you came to me; it is not for me to know that, but for another senseless, shameless girl who shamed her maiden room in the dark night, who sold her soul for mortal sin and could not school her frantic heart; and for my sorrowing tears to know it, and for him who, like a thief brags of another's woe and jeers at a maiden's heart!' I say it, and I could bear no more. I wept. . . . He said nothing; looked at me so that I trembled like a leaf. 'Listen to me,' said he, 'fair maid,' and his eyes burned strangely. 'It is not a vain word I say, I make you a solemn vow. As much happiness as you give me, so much will I be a gentleman, and if ever you do not love me—do not speak, do not drop a word, do not trouble, but stir only your sable eyebrow, turn your black eye, stir only your little finger and I will give you back your love with golden freedom; only, my proud, haughty beauty, then there will be an end to my life too.' And then all my flesh laughed at his words. . . ."

At this point Katerina's story was interrupted by deep emotion; she took breath, smiled at her new fancy and would have gone on, but suddenly her sparkling eyes met Ordynov's feverish gaze fixed on her. She started, would have said something, but the blood flooded her face. . . . She hid her face in her hands and fell upon the pillow as though in a swoon. Ordynov was quivering all over! An agonizing feeling, an unbearable, unaccountable agitation ran like poison through all his veins and grew with every word of Katerina's story; a hopeless yearning, a greedy and unendurable passion took possession of his imagination and troubled his feelings, but at the same time his heart was more and more oppressed by bitter, infinite sadness. At moments he longed to shriek to Katerina to be silent, longed to fling himself at her feet and beseech her by his tears to give him back his former agonies of love, his former pure, unquestioning yearning, and he regretted the tears that had long dried on his cheeks. There was an ache at his heart which was painfully oppressed by fever and could not give his tortured soul the relief of tears. He did not understand what Katerina was telling him, and his love was frightened of the feeling that excited the poor woman. He cursed his passion at that moment; it smothered him, it exhausted him, and he felt as though molten lead were running in his veins instead of blood.

"Ach! that is not my grief," said Katerina, suddenly raising her head. "What I have told you just now is not my sorrow," she went on in a voice that rang like copper from a sudden new feeling, while her heart was rent with secret, unshed tears. "That is not my grief, that is not my anguish, not my woe! What, what do I care for my mother, though I shall never have another mother in this world! What do I care that she cursed me in her last terrible hour? What do I care for my old golden life, for my warm room, for my maiden freedom? What do I care that I have sold myself to the evil one and abandoned my soul to the destroyer, that for the sake of happiness I have committed the unpardonable sin? Ach, that is not my grief, though in that great is my ruin! But what is bitter to me and rends my heart is that I am his shameless slave, that my shame and disgrace are dear to me, shameless as I am, but it is dear to my greedy heart to remember my sorrow as though it were joy and happiness; that is my grief, that there is no strength in it and no anger for my wrongs! . . ."

The poor creature gasped for breath and a convulsive, hysterical sob cut short her words, her hot, laboured breath burned her lips, her bosom heaved and sank and her eyes flashed with incomprehensible indignation. But her face was radiant with such fascination at that moment, every line, every muscle quivered with such a passionate flood of feeling, such insufferable, incredible beauty that Ordynov's black thoughts died away at once and the pure sadness in his soul was silenced. And his heart burned to be pressed to her heart and to be lost with it in frenzied emotion, to throb in harmony with the same storm, the same rush of infinite passion, and even to swoon with it. Katerina met Ordynov's troubled eyes and smiled so that his heart burned with redoubled fire. He scarcely knew what he was doing.

"Spare me, have pity on me," he whispered, controlling his trembling voice, bending down to her, leaning with his hand on her shoulder and looking close in her eyes, so close that their breathing was mingled in one. "You are killing me. I do not know your sorrow and my soul is troubled. . . . What is it to me what your heart is weeping over! Tell me what you want—I will do it. Come with me, let us go; do not kill me, do not murder me! . . ."

Katerina looked at him immovably, the tears dried on her burning cheeks. She wanted to interrupt him, to take his hand, tried to say something, but could not find the words. A strange smile came upon her lips, as though laughter were breaking through that smile.

"I have not told you all, then," she said at last in a broken voice; "only will you hear me, will you hear me, hot heart? Listen to your sister. You have learned little of her bitter grief. I would have told you how I lived a year with him, but I will not. . . . A year passed, he went away with his comrades down the river, and I was left with one he called his mother to wait for him in the harbour. I waited for him one month, two, and I met a young merchant, and I glanced at him and thought of my golden years gone by. 'Sister, darling,' said he, when he had spoken two words to me, 'I am Alyosha, your destined betrothed; the old folks betrothed us as children; you have forgotten me—think, I am from your parts.' 'And what do they say of me in your parts?' 'Folk's gossip says that you behaved dishonourably, forgot your maiden modesty, made friends with a brigand, a murderer,' Alyosha said, laughing. 'And what did you say of me?' 'I meant to say many things when I came here'— and his heart was troubled. 'I meant to say many things, but now that I have seen you my heart is dead within me, you have slain me,' he said. 'Buy my soul, too, take it, though you mock at my heart and my love, fair maiden. I am an orphan now, my own master, and my soul is my own, not another's. I have not sold it to any one, like somebody who has blotted out her memory; it's not enough to buy the heart, I give it for nothing, and it is clear it is a good bargain.' I laughed, and more than once, more than twice he talked to me; a whole month he lived on the place, gave up his merchandise, forsook his people and was all alone. I was sorry for his lonely tears. So I said to him one morning, 'Wait for me, Alyosha, lower down the harbour, as night comes on; I will go with you to your home, I am weary of my life, forlorn.' So night came on, I tied up a bundle and my soul ached and worked within me. Behold, my master walks in without word or warning. 'Good-day, let us go, there will be a storm on the river and the time will not wait.' I followed him; we came to the river and it was far to reach his mates. We look: a boat and one we knew rowing in it as though waiting for some one. 'Good-day, Alyosha; God be your help. Why, are you belated at the harbour, are you in haste to meet your vessels? Row me, good man, with the mistress, to our mates, to our place. I have let my boat go and I don't know how to swim.' 'Get in,' said Alyosha, and my whole soul swooned when I heard his voice. 'Get in with the mistress, too, the wind is for all, and in my bower there will be room for you, too.' We got in; it was a dark night, the stars were in hiding, the wind howled, the waves rose high and we rowed out a mile from shore—all three were silent.

"'It's a storm,' said my master, 'and it is a storm that bodes no good! I have never seen such a storm on the river in my life as is raging now! It is too much for our boat, it will not bear three!' 'No, it will not,' answered Alyosha, ' and one of us, it seems, turns out to be one too many,' he says, and his voice quivers like a harp-string. 'Well, Alyosha, I knew you as a little child, your father was my mate, we ate at each other's boards—tell me, Alyosha, can you reach the shore without the boat or will you perish for nothing, will you lose your life?' 'I cannot reach it. And you, too, good man, if it is your luck to have a drink of water, will you reach the shore or not?' 'I cannot reach it, it is the end for my soul. I cannot hold out against the stormy river! Listen, Katerina, my precious pearl! I remember such a night, but the waves were not tossing, the stars were shining, and the moon was bright. . . . I simply want to ask you, have you forgotten?' 'I remember,' said I 'Well, since you have not forgotten it, well, you have not forgotten the compact when a bold man told a fair maiden to take back her freedom from one unloved—eh?' ' 'No, I have not forgotten that either,' I said, more dead than alive. 'Ah, you have not forgotten! Well, now we are in hard case in the boat. Has not his hour come for one of us? Tell me, my own, tell me my dove, coo to us like a dove your tender word . . .'"

"I did not say my word then," whispered Katerina, turning pale. . .

"Katerina!" A hoarse, hollow voice resounded above them. Ordynov started. In the doorway stood Murin. He was barely covered with a fur rug, pale as death, and he was gazing at them with almost senseless eyes. Katerina turned paler and paler and she, too, gazed fixedly at him, as though spellbound.

"Come to me, Katerina," whispered the sick man, in a voice hardly audible, and went out of the room. Katerina still gazed fixedly into the air, as though the old man had still been standing before her. But suddenly the blood rushed glowing into her pale cheeks and she slowly got up from the bed. Ordynov remembered their first meeting.

"Till to-morrow then, my tears!" she said, laughing strangely; "till to-morrow! Remember at what point I stopped: 'Choose between the two; which is dear or not dear to you, fair maid!' Will you remember, will you wait for one night?" she repeated, laying her hand on his shoulder and looking at him tenderly.

"Katerina, do not go, do not go to your ruin! He is mad," whispered Ordynov, trembling for her.

"Katerina!" he heard through the partition.

"What? Will he murder me? no fear!" Katerina answered, laughing. "Good-night to you, my precious heart, my warm dove, my brother!" she said, tenderly pressing his head to her bosom, while tears bedewed her face. "Those are my last tears. Sleep away your sorrow, my darling, wake to-morrow to joy. And she kissed him passionately.

"Katerina, Katerina!" whispered Ordynov, falling on his knees before her and trying to stop her. "Katerina!"

She turned round, nodded to him, smiling, and went out of the room. Ordynov heard her go in to Murin; he held his breath, listening, but heard not a sound more. The old man was silent or perhaps unconscious again. . . . He would have gone in to her there, but his legs staggered under him. . . . He sank exhausted on the bed. . .

II

For a long while he could not find out what the time was when he woke. Whether it was the twilight of dawn or of evening, it was still dark in his room. He could not decide how long he had slept, but felt that his sleep was not healthy sleep. Coming to himself, he passed his hand over his face as though shaking off sleep and the visions of the night. But when he tried to step on the floor he felt as though his whole body were shattered, and his exhausted limbs refused to obey him. His head ached and was going round, and he was alternately shivering and feverish. Memory returned with consciousness and his heart quivered when in one instant he lived through, in memory, the whole of the past night. His heart beat as violently in response to his thoughts, his sensations were as burning, as fresh, as though not a night, not long hours, but one minute had passed since Katerina had gone away. He felt as though his eyes were still wet with tears—or were they new, fresh tears that rushed like a spring from his burning soul? And, strange to say, his agonies were even sweet to him, though he dimly felt all over that he could not endure such violence of feeling again. There was a moment when he was almost conscious of death, and was ready to meet it as a welcome guest; his sensations were so overstrained, his passion surged up with such violence on waking, such ecstasy took possession of his soul that life, quickened by its intensity, seemed on the point of breaking, of being shattered, of flickering out in one minute and being quenched for ever. Almost at that instant, as though in answer to his anguish, in answer to his quivering heart, the familiar mellow, silvery voice of Katerina rang out-like that inner music known to man's soul in hours of joy, in hours of tranquil happiness. Close beside him, almost over his pillow, began a song, at first soft and melancholy . . . her voice rose and fell, dying away abruptly as though hiding in itself, and tenderly crooning over its anguish of unsatisfied, smothered desire hopelessly concealed in the grieving heart; then again it flowed into a nightingale's trills and, quivering and glowing with unrestrained passion, melted into a perfect sea of ecstasy, a sea of mighty, boundless sound, like the first moment of the bliss of love.

Ordynov distinguished the words, too. They were simple, sincere, composed long ago with direct, calm, pure, clear feeling, but he forgot them, he heard only the sounds. Through the simple, naïve verses of the song flashed other words resounding with all the yearning that filled his bosom, responding to the most secret subtleties of his passion, which he could not comprehend though they echoed to him clearly with full consciousness of it. And at one moment he heard the last moan of a heart swooning helplessly in passion, then he heard the joy of a will and a spirit breaking its chains and rushing brightly and freely into the boundless ocean of unfettered love. Then he heard the first vow of the beloved, with fragrant shame at the first blush on her face, with prayers, with tears, with mysterious timid murmuring; then the passion of the Bacchante, proud and rejoicing in its strength, unveiled, undisguised, turning her drunken eyes about her with a ringing laugh . . .

Ordynov could not endure the end of the song, and he got up from the bed. The song at once died away.

"Good-morning and good-day are over, my beloved," Katerina's voice rang out, "Good-evening to you; get up, come in to us, wake up to bright joy; we expect you. I and the master, both good people, your willing servants, quench hatred with love, if your heart is still resentful. Say a friendly word!" . . .

Ordynov had already gone out of his room at her first call and scarcely realized that he was going into the landlord's bedroom. The door opened before him and, bright as sunshine, the golden smile of his strange landlady flashed upon him. At that instant, he saw, he heard no one but her. In one moment his whole life, his whole joy, melted into one thing in his heart—the bright image of his Katerina.

"Two dawns have passed," she said, giving him her hands, "since we said farewell; the second is dying now—look out of the window. Like the two dawns in the soul of a maiden," Katerina added, laughing. "The one that flushes her face with its first shame, when first her lonely maiden heart speaks in her bosom, while the other, when a maiden forgets her first shame, glows like fire, stifles her maiden heart, and drives the red blood to her face. . . . Come, come into our home, good young man! Why do you stand in the doorway? Honour and love to you, and a greeting from the master!"

With a laugh ringing like music, she took Ordynov's hand and led him into the room. His heart was overwhelmed with timidity-All the fever, all the fire raging in his bosom was quenched and died down in one instant, and for one instant he dropped his eyes in confusion and was afraid to look at her. He felt that she was so marvellously beautiful that his heart could not endure her burning eyes. He had never seen his Katerina like this. For the first time laughter and gaiety were sparkling on her face, and drying the mournful tears on her black eyelashes. His hand trembled in her hand. And if he had raised his eyes he would have seen that Katerina, with a triumphant smile, had fastened her clear eyes on his face, which was clouded with confusion and passion.

"Get up, old man," she said at last, as though waking up; "say a word of welcome to our guest, a guest who is like a brother! Get up, you proud, unbending old man; get up, now, take your guest by his white hand and make him sit down to the table."

Ordynov raised his eyes and seemed only then to come to himself. Only then he thought of Murin. The old man's eyes, looking as though dimmed by the approach of death, were staring at him fixedly; and with a pang in his heart he remembered those eyes glittering at him last time from black overhanging brows contracted as now with pain and anger. There was a slight dizziness in his head. He looked round him and only then realized everything clearly and distinctly. Murin was still lying on the bed, but he was partly dressed and had already been up and out that morning. As before, he had a red kerchief tied round his neck, he had slippers on his feet. His attack was evidently over, only his face was still terribly pale and yellow. Katerina was standing by his bed, her hand leaning on the table, watching them both intently. But the smile of welcome did not leave her face. It seemed as though everything had been done at a sign from her.

"Yes! it's you," said Murin, raising himself up and sitting on the bed. "You are my lodger. I must beg your pardon, sir; I have sinned and wronged you all unknowingly, playing tricks with my gun the other day. Who could tell that you, too, were stricken by grievous sickness? It happens to me at times," he added in a hoarse, ailing voice, frowning and unconsciously looking away from Ordynov. "My trouble comes upon me like a thief in the night without knocking at the gate! I almost thrust a knife into her bosom the other day . . ." he brought out, nodding towards Katerina. "I am ill, a fit comes, seizes me—well, that's enough. Sit down—you will be our guest."

Ordynov was still staring at him intently.

"Sit down, sit down!" the old man shouted impatiently; "sit down, if that will please her! So you are brother and sister, born of the same mother! You are as fond of one another as lovers!"

Ordynov sat down.

"You see what a fine sister you've got," the old man went on, laughing, and he showed two rows of white, perfectly sound, teeth. "Be fond of one another, my dears. Is your sister beautiful, sir? Tell me, answer! Come, look how her cheeks are burning; come, look round, sing the praises of her beauty to all the world, show that your heart is aching for her."

Ordynov frowned and looked angrily at the old man, who flinched under his eyes. A blind fury surged up in Ordynov's heart. By some animal instinct he felt near him a mortal foe. He could not understand what was happening to him, his reason refused to serve him.

"Don't look," said a voice behind him.

Ordynov looked round.

"Don't look, don't look, I tell you, if the devil is tempting you; have pity on your love," said Katerina, laughing, and suddenly from behind she covered his eyes with her hands; then at once took away her hands and hid her own face in them. But the colour in her face seemed to show through her fingers. She removed her hands and, still glowing like fire, tried to meet their laughter and inquisitive eyes brightly and without a tremor. But both looked at her in silence—Ordynov with the stupefication of love, as though it were the first time such terrible beauty had stabbed his heart; the old man coldly and attentively. Nothing was to be seen in his pale face, except that his lips turned blue and quivered faintly.

Katerina went up to the old man, no longer laughing, and began clearing away the books, papers, inkstand, everything that was on the table and putting them all on the window-sill. Her breathing was hurried and uneven, and from time to time she drew an eager breath as though her heart were oppressed. Her full bosom heaved and fell like a wave on the seashore. She dropped her eyes and her pitchblack eyelashes gleamed on her bright cheeks like sharp needles. . . .

"A maiden queen," said the old man.

"My sovereign!" whispered Ordynov, quivering all over. He came to his senses, feeling the old man's eyes upon him—his glance flashed upon him for an instant like lightning—greedy spiteful, coldly contemptuous. Ordynov would have got up from his seat but some unseen power seemed to fetter his legs. He sat down again. At times he pinched his hand as though not believing in reality. He felt as though he was being strangled by a nightmare, and as though his eyes were still closed in a miserable feverish sleep. But, strange to say, he did not want to wake up!

Katerina took the old cloth off the table, then opened a chest, took out of it a sumptuous cloth embroidered in gold and bright silks and put it on the table; then she took out of the cupboard an old-fashioned ancestral-looking casket, set it in the middle of the table and took out of it three silver goblets—one for the master, one for the visitor, and one for herself; then with a grave, almost pensive air, she looked at the old man and at the visitor.

"Is one of us dear to some one, or not dear," she said. "If any one is not dear to some one he is dear to me, and shall drink my goblet with me. Each of you is dear to me as my own brother: so let us all drink to love and concord."

"Drink and drown dark fancies in the wine," said the old man, in a changed voice. "Pour it out, Katerina."

"Do you bid me pour?" asked Katerina, looking at Ordynov.

Ordynov held out his goblet in silence.

"Stay! If one has a secret and a fancy, may his wishes come true!" said the old man, raising his goblet. All clinked their goblets and drank.

"Let me drink now with you, old man," said Katerina, turning to the landlord. "Let us drink if your heart is kindly to me! Let us drink to past happiness, let us send a greeting to the years we have spent, let us celebrate our happiness with heart and with love. Bid me fill your goblet if your heart is warm to me."

"Your wine is strong, my love, but you scarcely wet your lips!" said the old man, laughing and holding out his goblet again.

"Well, I will sip it, but you drink it to the bottom . . . why live, old man, brooding on gloomy thoughts; gloomy thoughts only make the heart ache! Thought calls for sorrow; with happiness one can live without thinking; drink, old man," she went on; "drown your thoughts."

"A great deal of sorrow must have fermented within you, since you arm yourself against it like this! So you want to make an end of it all at once, my white dove. I drink with you, Katya! And have you a sorrow, sir, if you allow me ask?"

"If I have, I keep it to myself," muttered Ordynov, keeping his eyes fixed on Katerina.

"Do you hear, old man? For a long while I did not know myself, did not remember; but the time came, I remembered all and recalled it; all that has passed I have passed through again in my unsatisfied soul."

"Yes, it is grievous if one begins looking into the past only," said the old man dreamily. "What is past is like wine that is drunk! What happiness is there in the past? The coat is worn out, and away with it."

"One must get a new one," Katerina chimed in with a strained laugh, while two big tears like diamonds hung on her eyelashes."One cannot live down a lifetime in one minute and a girl's heart is eager for life—there is no keeping pace with it. Do you understand, old man? Look. I have buried my tear in your goblet."

"And did you buy much happiness with your sorrow?" said Ordynov—and his voice quivered with emotion.

"So you must have a great deal of your own for sale," answered the old man, "that you put your spoke in unasked," and he laughed a spiteful, noiseless laugh, looking insolently at Ordynov.

"What I have sold it for, I have had," answered Katerina in a voice that sounded vexed and offended. "One thinks it much, another little. One wants to give all to take nothing, another promises nothing and yet the submissive heart follows him! Do not you reproach any one," she went on, looking sadly at Ordynov. "One man is like this, and another is different, and as though one knew why the soul yearns towards any one! Fill your goblet, old man. Drink to the happiness of your dear daughter, your meek, obedient slave, as I was when first I knew you. Raise your goblet!"

"So be it! Fill yours, too!" said the old man, taking the wine.

"Stay, old man! Put off drinking, and let us say a word first! . . ."

Katerina put her elbows on the table and looked intently, with passionate, kindling eyes, at the old man. A strange determination gleamed in her eyes. But all her movements were calm, her gestures were abrupt, unexpected, rapid. She was all as if on fire, and it was marvellous; but her beauty seemed to grow with her emotion, her animation; her hurried breath slightly inflating her nostrils, floated from her lips, half-opened in a smile which showed two rows of teeth white and even as pearls. Her bosom heaved, her coil of hair, twisted three times round her head, fell carelessly over her left ear and covered part of her glowing cheek, drops of sweat came out on her temples.

"Tell my fortune, old man; tell my fortune, my father, before you drown your mind in drink. Here is my white palm for you—not for nothing do the folks call you a wizard. You have studied by the book and know all of the black art! Look, old man, tell me all my pitiful fate; only mind you don't tell a lie! Come, tell me as you know it— will there be happiness for your daughter, or will you not forgive her, but call down upon her path an evil, sorrowful fate? Tell me whether I shall have a warm corner for my home, or, like a bird of passage, shall be seeking among good people for a home—a lonely orphan all my life. Tell me who is my enemy, who is preparing love for me, who is plotting against me; tell me, will my warm young heart open its life in solitude and languish to the end, or will it find itself a mate and beat joyfully in tune with it till new sorrow comes! Tell me for once, old man, in what blue sky, beyond far seas and forests, my bright falcon lives. And is he keenly searching for his mate, and is he waiting lovingly, and will he love me fondly; will he soon be tired of me, will he deceive me or not deceive me, and, once for all and altogether, tell me for the last time, old man, am I long to while away the time with you, to sit in a comfortless corner, to read dark books; and when am I, old man, to bow low to you, to say farewell for good and all, to thank you for your bread and salt, for giving me to drink and eat, for telling me your tales? . . . But mind, tell all the truth, do not lie. The time has come, stand up for yourself."

Her excitement grew greater and greater up to the last word, when suddenly her voice broke with emotion as though her heart were carried away by some inner tempest. Her eyes flashed, and her upper lip faintly quivered. A spiteful jeer could be heard hiding like a snake under every word, but yet there was the ring of tears in her laughter. She bent across the table to the old man and gazed with eager intentness into his lustreless eyes. Ordynov heard her heart suddenly begin beating when she finished; he cried out with ecstasy when he glanced at her, and was getting up from the bench. But a flitting momentary glance from the old man riveted him to his seat again. A strange mingling of contempt, mocking, impatient, angry uneasiness and at the same time sly, spiteful curiosity gleamed in his passing momentary glance, which every time made Ordynov shudder and filled his heart with annoyance, vexation and helpless anger.

Thoughtfully and with a sort of mournful curiosity the old man looked at his Katerina. His heart was stung, words had been uttered. But not an eyebrow stirred upon his face! He only smiled when she finished.

"You want to know a great deal at once, my full-fledged nestling, my fluttering bird! Better fill me a deep goblet! and let us drink first to peace and goodwill; or I may spoil my forecast, through some one's black evil eye. Mighty is the devil! Sin is never far off!"

He raised his goblet and drank. The more wine he drank, the paler he grew. His eyes burned like red coals. Evidently the feverish light of them, and the sudden deathlike blueness of his face were signs that another fit was imminent. The wine was strong, so that after emptying one goblet Ordynov's sight grew more and more blurred. His feverishly inflamed blood could bear no more: it rushed to his heart, troubled and dimmed his reason. His uneasiness grew more and more intense. To relieve his growing excitement, he filled his goblet and sipped it again, without knowing what he was doing, and the blood raced even more rapidly through his veins. He was as though in delirium, and, straining his attention to the utmost, he could hardly follow what was passing between his strange landlord and landlady.

The old man knocked his goblet with a ringing sound against the table.

"Fill it, Katerina!" he cried, " fill it again, bad daughter, fill it to the brim! Lay the old man in peace, and have done with him! That's it, pour out more, pour it out, my beauty! Let us drink together! Why have you drunk so little? Or have my eyes deceived me? . . ."

Katerina made him some answer, but Ordynov could not hear quite what she said: the old man did not let her finish; he caught hold of her hand as though he were incapable of restraining all that was weighing on his heart, His face was pale, his eyes at one moment were dim, at the next were flashing with fire; his lips quivered and turned white, and in an uneven, troubled voice, in which at moments there was a flash of strange ecstasy, he said to her—

"Give me your little hand, my beauty! Let me tell your fortune. I will tell the whole truth. I am truly a wizard; so you are not mistaken, Katerina! Your golden heart said truly that I alone am its wizard, and will not hide the truth from it, the simple, girlish heart! But one thing you don't see: it's not for me, a wizard, to teach you wisdom! Wisdom is not what a maiden wants, and she hears the whole truth, yet seems not to know, not to understand! Her head is a subtle serpent, though her heart is melting in tears. She will find out for herself, will thread her way between troubles, will keep her cunning will! Something she can win by sense, and where she cannot win by sense she will dazzle by beauty, will intoxicate men's minds with her black eye—beauty conquers strength, even the heart of iron will be rent asunder! Will you have grief and sorrow? Heavy is the sorrow of man! but trouble is not for the weak heart, trouble is close friends with the strong heart; stealthily it sheds a bloody tear, but does not go begging to good people for shameful comfort: your grief, girl, is like a print in the sand—the rain washes it away, the sun dries it, the stormy wind lifts it and blows it away. Let me tell you more, let me tell your fortune. Whoever loves you, you will be a slave to him, you will bind your freedom yourself, you will give yourself in pledge and will not take yourself back, you will not know how to cease to love in due time, you will sow a grain and your destroyer will take back a whole ear! My tender child, my little golden head, you buried your pearl of a tear in my goblet, but you could not be content with that—at once you shed a hundred; you uttered no more sweet words, and boasted of your sad life! And there was no need for you to grieve over it—the tear, the dew of heaven! It will come back to you with interest, your pearly tear, in the woeful night when cruel sorrow, evil fancies will gnaw your heart—then for that same tear another's tear will drop upon your warm heart—not a warm tear but a tear of blood, like molten lead; it will turn your white bosom to blood, and until the dreary, heavy morning that comes on gloomy days, you will toss in your little bed, shedding your heart's blood and will not heal your fresh wound till another dawn. Fill my goblet, Katerina, fill it again, my dove; fill it for my sage counsel, and no need to waste more words." His voice grew weak and trembling, sobs seemed on the point of breaking from his bosom, he poured out the wine and greedily drained another goblet. Then he brought the goblet down on the table again with a bang. His dim eyes once more gleamed with flame.

"Ah! Live as you may!" he shouted; "what's past is gone and done with. Fill up the heavy goblet, fill it up, that it may smite the rebellious head from its shoulders, that the whole soul may be dead with it! Lay me out for the long night that has no morning and let my memory vanish altogether. What is drunk is lived and done with. So the merchant's wares have grown stale, have lain by too long, he must give them away for nothing! but the merchant would not of his free will have sold it below its price. The blood of his foe should be spilt and the innocent blood should be shed too, and that customer should have laid down his lost soul into the bargain! Fill my goblet, fill it again, Katerina."

But the hand that held the goblet seemed to stiffen and did not move; his breathing was laboured and difficult, his head sank back. For the last time he fixed his lustreless eyes on Ordynov, but his eyes, too, grew dim at last, and his eyelids dropped as though they were made of lead. A deadly pallor overspread his face . . . For some time his lips twitched and quivered as though still trying to articulate— and suddenly a big hot tear hung on his eyelash, broke and slowly ran down his pale cheek. . .

Ordynov could bear no more. He got up and, reeling, took a step forward, went up to Katerina and clutched her hand. But she seemed not to notice him and did not even glance at him, as though she did not recognize him. . . .

She, too, seemed to have lost consciousness, as though one thought, one fixed idea had entirely absorbed her. She sank on the bosom of the sleeping old man, twined her white arm round his neck, and gazed with glowing, feverish eyes as though they were riveted on him. She did not seem to feel Ordynov taking her hand. At last she turned her head towards him, and bent upon him a prolonged searching gaze. It seemed as though at last she understood, and a bitter, astonished smile came wearily, as it were painfully, on her lips. . . .

"Go away, go away," she whispered; "you are drunk and wicked, you are not a guest for me . . ." then she turned again to the old man and riveted her eyes upon him.

She seemed as it were gloating over every breath he took and soothing his slumber with her eyes. She seemed afraid to breathe, checking her full throbbing heart, and there was such frenzied admiration in her face that at once despair, fury and insatiable anger seized upon Ordynov's spirit. . . .

"Katerina! Katerina!" he called, seizing her hand as though in a vice.

A look of pain passed over her face; she raised her head again, and looked at him with such mockery, with such contemptuous haughtiness, that he could scarcely stand upon his feet. Then she pointed to the sleeping old man and—as though all his enemy's mockery had passed into her eyes, she bent again a taunting, glance at Ordynov that sent an icy shiver to his heart.

"What? He will murder me, I suppose?" said Ordynov, beside himself with fury. Some demon seemed to whisper in his ear that he understood her . . . and his whole heart laughed at Katerina's fixed idea.

"I will buy you, my beauty, from your merchant, if you want my soul; no fear, he won't kill me! . . ." A fixed laugh, that froze Ordynov's whole being, remained upon Katerina's face. Its boundless irony rent his heart. Not knowing what he was doing, hardly conscious, he leaned against the wall and took from a nail the old man's expensive old-fashioned knife. A look of amazement seemed to come into Katerina's face, but at the same time anger and contempt were reflected with the same force in her eyes. Ordynov turned sick, looking at her . . . he felt as though some one were thrusting, urging his frenzied hand to madness. He drew out the knife . . . Katerina watched him, motionless, holding her breath. . . .

He glanced at the old man.

At that moment he fancied that one of the old man's eyes opened and looked at him, laughing. Their eyes met. For some minutes Ordynov gazed at him fixedly. . . . Suddenly he fancied that the old man's whole face began laughing and that a diabolical, soul-freezing chuckle resounded at last through the room. A hideous, dark thought crawled like a snake into his head. He shuddered; the knife fell from his hands and dropped with a clang upon the floor. Katerina uttered a shriek as though awaking from oblivion, from a nightmare, from a heavy, immovable, vision. . . . The old man, very pale, slowly got up from the bed and angrily kicked the knife into the comer of the room; Katerina stood pale, deathlike, immovable; her eyelids were closing; her face was convulsed by a vague, insufferable pain; she hid her face in her hands and, with a shriek that rent the heart, sank almost breathless at the old man's feet. . . .

"Alyosha, Alyosha!" broke from her gasping bosom.

The old man seized her in his powerful arms and almost crushed her on his breast. But when she hid her head upon his heart, every feature in the old man's face worked with such undisguised, shameless laughter that Ordynov's whole soul was overwhelmed with horror. Deception, calculation, cold, jealous tyranny and horror at the poor broken heart— that was what he read in that laugh, that shamelessly threw off all disguise.

"She is mad!" he whispered, quivering like a leaf, and, numb with terror, he ran out of the flat.

III

When, at eight o'clock next morning, Ordynov, pale and agitated and still dazed from the excitement of that day, opened Yaroslav Ilyitch's door (he went to see him though he could not have said why) he staggered back in amazement and stood petrified in the doorway on seeing Murin in the room. The old man, even paler than Ordynov, seemed almost too ill to stand up; he would not sit down, however, though Yaroslav Ilyitch, highly delighted at the visit, invited him to do so. Yaroslav Ilyitch, too, cried out in surprise at seeing Ordynov, but almost at once his delight died away, and he was quite suddenly overtaken by embarrassment halfway between the table and the chair next it. It was evident that he did not know what to say or to do, and was fully conscious of the impropriety of sucking at his pipe and of leaving his visitor to his own devices at such a difficult moment. And yet (such was his confusion) he did go on pulling at his pipe with all his might and indeed with a sort of enthusiasm. Ordynov went into the room at last. He flung a cursory glance at Murin, a look flitted over the old man's face, something like the malicious smile of the day before, which even now set Ordynov shuddering with indignation. All hostility, however, vanished at once and was smoothed away, and the old man's face assumed a perfectly unapproachable and reserved air. He dropped a very low bow to his lodger. . . . The scene brought Ordynov to a sense of reality at last. Eager to understand the position of affairs, he looked intently at Yaroslav Ilyitch, who began to be uneasy and flustered.

"Come in, come in," he brought out at last. "Come in, most precious Vassily Mihalitch; honour me with your presence, and put a stamp of . . . on all these ordinary objects . . ." said Yaroslav Ilyitch, pointing towards a corner of the room, flushing like a crimson rose; confused and angry that even his most exalted sentences floundered and missed fire, he moved the chair with a loud noise into the very middle of the room.

"I hope I'm not hindering you, Yaroslav Ilyitch," said Ordynov. "I wanted . . . for two minutes. . . ."

"Upon my word! As though you could hinder me, Vassily Mihalitch; but let me offer you a cup of tea. Hey, servant. . . I am sure you, too, will not refuse a cup!"

Murin nodded, signifying thereby that he would not.

Yaroslav Ilyitch shouted to the servant who came in, sternly demanded another three glasses, then sat down beside Ordynov. For some time he turned his head like a plaster kitten to right and to left, from Murin to Ordynov, and from Ordynov to Murin His position was extremely unpleasant. He evidently wanted to say something, to his notions extremely delicate, for one side at any rate. But for all his efforts he was totally unable to utter a word . . . Ordynov, too, seemed in perplexity. There was a moment when both began speaking at once. . . . Murin, silent, watching them both with curiosity, slowly opened his mouth and showed all his teeth. . . .

"I've come to tell you," Ordynov said suddenly, "that, owing to a most unpleasant circumstance, I am obliged to leave my lodging, and . . ."

"Fancy, what a strange circumstance!" Yaroslav Ilyitch interrupted suddenly. "I confess I was utterly astounded when this worthy old man told me this morning of your intention. But . . ."

"*He* told you," said Ordynov, looking at Murin with surprise.

Murin stroked his beard and laughed in his sleeve.

"Yes," Yaroslav Ilyitch rejoined; "though I may have made a mistake. But I venture to say for you—I can answer for it on my honour that there was not a shadow of anything derogatory to you in this worthy old man's words . . ."

Here Yaroslav Ilyitch blushed and controlled his emotion with an effort. Murin, after enjoying to his heart's content the discomfiture of the other two men, took a step forward.

"It is like this, your honour," he began, bowing politely to Ordynov: "His honour made bold to take a little trouble on your behalf. As it seems, sir—you know yourself—the mistress and I, that is, we would be glad, freely and heartily, and we would not have made bold to say a word . . . but the way I live, you know yourself, you see for yourself, sir! Of a truth, the Lord barely keeps us alive, for which we pray His holy will; else you see yourself, sir, whether it is for me to make lamentation." Here Murin again wiped his beard with his sleeve.

Ordynov almost turned sick.

"Yes, yes, I told you about him, myself; he is ill, that is this *malheur*. I should like to express myself in French but, excuse me, I don't speak French quite easily; that is . . ."

"Quite so . . ."

"Quite so, that is . . ."

Ordynov and Yaroslav Ilyitch made each other a half bow, each a little on one side of his chair, and both covered their confusion with an apologetic laugh. The practical Yaroslav Ilyitch recovered at once.

"I have been questioning this honest man minutely," he began. "He has been telling me that the illness of this woman. . . ." Here the delicate Yaroslav Ilyitch, probably wishing to conceal a slight embarrassment that showed itself in his face, hurriedly looked at Murin with inquiry.

"Yes, of our mistress . . ."

The refined Yaroslav Ilyitch did not insist further.

"The mistress, that is, your former landlady; I don't know how . . . but there! She is an afflicted woman, you see . . . She says that she is hindering you . . . in your studies, and he himself . . . you concealed from me one important circumstance, Vassily Mihalitch!"

"What?"

"About the gun," Yaroslav Ilyitch brought out, almost whispering in the most indulgent tone with the millionth fraction of reproach softly ringing in his friendly tenor.

"But," he added hurriedly, "he has told me all about it. And you acted nobly in overlooking his involuntary wrong to you. I swear I saw tears in his eyes."

Yaroslav Ilyitch flushed again, his eyes shone and he shifted in his chair with emotion.

"I, that is, we, sir, that is, your honour, I, to be sure, and my mistress remember you in our prayers," began Murin, addressing Ordynov and looking at him while Yaroslav Ilyitch overcame his habitual agitation; "and you know yourself, sir, she is a sick, foolish woman; my legs will hardly support me . . ."

"Yes, I am ready," Ordynov said impatiently; "please, that's enough, I am going directly . . ."

"No, that is, sir, we are very grateful for your kindness" (Murin made a very low bow); "that is not what I meant to tell you, sir; I wanted to say a word—you see, sir, she came to me almost from her home, that is from far, as the saying is, beyond the seventh water—do not scorn our humble talk, sir, we are ignorant folk—and from a tiny child she has been like this! A sick brain, hasty, she grew up in the forest, grew up a peasant, all among bargemen and factory hands; and then their house must burn down; her mother, sir, was burnt, her father burnt to death—I daresay there is no knowing what she'll tell you . . . I don't meddle, but the Chir—chir-urgi-cal Council examined her at Moscow. You see, sir, she's quite incurable, that's what it is. I am all that's left her, and she lives with me. We live, we pray to God and trust in the Almighty; I never cross her in anything."

Ordynov's face changed. Yaroslav Ilyitch looked first at one, then at the other.

"But, that is not what I wanted to say . . . no!" Murin corrected himself, shaking his head gravely. "She is, so to say, such a featherhead, such a whirligig, such a loving, headstrong creature, she's always wanting a sweetheart—if you will pardon my saying so—and some one to love; it's on that she's mad. I amuse her with fairy tales, I do my best at it. I saw, sir, how she—forgive my foolish words, sir," Murin went on, bowing and wiping his beard with his sleeve—"how she made friends with you; you, so to say, your excellency, were desirous to approach her with a view to love."

Yaroslav Ilyitch flushed crimson, and looked reproachfully at Murin. Ordynov could scarcely sit still in his seat.

"No . . . that is not it, sir . . . I speak simply, sir, I am a peasant, I am at your service. . . . Of course, we are ignorant folk, we are your servants, sir," he brought out, bowing low; "and my wife and I will pray with all our hearts for your honour. . . . What do we need? To be strong and have enough to eat—we do not repine; but what am I to do, sir; put my head in the noose? You know yourself, sir, what life is and will have pity on us; but what will it be like, sir, if she has a lover, too! . . . Forgive my rough words, sir; I am a peasant, sir, and you are a gentleman. . . . You're a young man, your excellency, proud and hasty, and she, you know yourself, sir, is a little child with no sense— it's easy for her to fall into sin. She's a buxom lass, rosy and sweet, while I am an old man always ailing. Well, the devil, it seems, has tempted, your honour. I always flatter her with fairy tales, I do indeed; I flatter her; and how we will pray, my wife and I, for your honour! How we will pray! And what is she to you, your excellency, if she is pretty? Still she is a simple woman, an unwashed peasant woman, a foolish rustic maid, a match for a peasant like me. It is not for a gentleman like you, sir, to be friends with peasants! But she and I will pray to God for your honour; how we will pray!"

Here Murin bowed very low and for a long while remained with his back bent, continually wiping his beard with his sleeve.

Yaroslav Ilyitch did not know where he was standing.

"Yes, this good man," he observed in conclusion, "spoke to me of some undesirable incidents; I did not venture to believe him, Vassily Mihalitch, I heard that you were still ill," he interrupted hurriedly, looking at Ordynov in extreme embarrassment, with eyes full of tears of emotion.

"Yes, how much do I owe you?" Ordynov asked Murin hurriedly.

"What are you saying, your honour? Give over. Why, we are not Judases. Why, you are insulting us, sir, we should be ashamed, sir. Have I and my good woman offended you?"

"But this is really strange, my good man; why, his honour took the room from you; don't you feel that you are insulting him by refusing?" Yaroslav Ilyitch interposed, thinking it his duty to show Murin the strangeness and indelicacy of his conduct.

"But upon my word, sir! What do you mean, sir? What did we not do to please your honour? Why, we tried our very best, we did our utmost, upon my word! Give over, sir, give over your honour. Christ have mercy upon you! Why, are we infidels or what? You might have lived, you might have eaten our humble fare with us and welcome; you might have lain there—we'd have said nothing against it, and we wouldn't have dropped a word; but the evil one tempted you. I am an afflicted man and my mistress is afflicted—what is one to do? There was no one to wait on you, or we would have been glad, glad from our hearts. And how the mistress and I will pray for your honour, how we will pray for you."

Murin bowed down from the waist. Tears came into Yaroslav Ilyitch's delighted eyes. He looked with enthusiasm at Ordynov.

"What a generous trait, isn't it! What sacred hospitality is to be found in the Russian people."

Ordynov looked wildly at Yaroslav Ilyitch.

He was almost terrified and scrutinized him from head to foot.

"Yes, indeed, sir, we do honour hospitality; we do honour it indeed, sir," Murin asserted, covering his beard with his whole sleeve. "Yes, indeed, the thought just came to me; we'd have welcomed you as a guest, sir, by God! we would," he went on, approaching Ordynov; "and I had nothing against it; another day I would have said nothing, nothing at all; but sin is a sore snare and my mistress is ill. Ah, if it were not for the mistress! Here, if I had been alone, for instance; how glad I would have been of your honour, how I would have waited upon you, wouldn't I have waited upon you! Whom should we respect if not your honour? I'd have healed you of your sickness, I know the art. . . . You should have been our guest, upon my word you should, that is a great word with us! . . ."

"Yes, really; is there such an art?" observed Yaroslav Ilyitch . . . and broke off.

Ordynov had done Yaroslav Ilyitch injustice when, just before, he had looked him up and down with wild amazement.

He was, of course, a very honest and honourable person, but now he understood everything and it must be owned his position was a very difficult one. He wanted to explode, as it is called, with laughter! If he had been alone with Ordynov—two such friends—Yaroslav Ilyitch would, of course, have given way to an immoderate outburst of gaiety without attempting to control himself. He would, however, have done this in a gentlemanly way He would after laughing have pressed Ordynov's hand with feeling, would genuinely and justly have assured him that he felt double respect for him and that he could make allowances in every case . . . and, of course, would have made no reference to his youth. But as it was, with his habitual delicacy of feeling, he was in a most difficult position and scarcely knew what to do with himself. . . .

"Arts, that is decoctions," Murin added. A quiver passed over his face at Yaroslav Ilyitch's tactless exclamation. "What I should say, sir, in my peasant foolishness," he went on, taking another step forward, "you've read too many books, sir; as the Russian saying is among us peasants, 'Wit has overstepped wisdom.' . . ."

"Enough," said Yaroslav Ilyitch sternly.

"I am going," said Ordynov. "I thank you, Yaroslav Ilyitch. I will come, I will certainly come and see you," he said in answer to the redoubled civilities of Yaroslav Ilyitch, who was unable to detain him further. "Good-bye, good-bye."

"Good-bye, your honour, good-bye, sir; do not forget us, visit us, poor sinners."

Ordynov heard nothing more—he went out like one distraught. He could bear no more, he felt shattered, his mind was numb, he dimly felt that he was overcome by illness, but cold despair reigned in his soul, and he was only conscious of a vague pain crushing, wearing, gnawing at his breast; he longed to die at that minute. His legs were giving way under him and he sat down by the fence, taking no notice of the passing people, nor of the crowd that began to collect around him, nor of the questions, nor the exclamations of the curious. But, suddenly, in the multitude of voices, he heard the voice of Murin above him. Ordynov raised his head. The old man really was standing before him, his pale face was thoughtful and dignified, he was quite a different man from the one who had played the coarse farce at Yaroslav Ilyitch's. Ordynov got up. Murin took his arm and led him out of the crowd. "You want to get your belongings," he said, looking sideways at Ordynov. "Don't grieve, sir," cried Murin. "You are young, why grieve? . . ."

Ordynov made no reply.

"Are you offended, sir? . . . To be sure you are very angry now . . . but you have no cause; every man guards his own goods!"

"I don't know you," said Ordynov; "I don't want to know your secrets. But she, she! . . ." he brought out, and the tears rushed in streams from his eyes. The wind blew them one after another from his cheeks . . . Ordynov wiped them with his hand; his gesture, his eyes, the involuntary movement of his blue lips all looked like madness.

"I've told you already," said Murin, knitting his brows, "that she is crazy! What crazed her? . . . Why need you know? But to me, even so, she is dear! I've loved her more than my life and I'll give her up to no one. Do you understand now?"

There was a momentary gleam of fire in Ordynov's eyes.

"But why have I . . .? Why have I as good as lost my life? Why does my heart ache? Why did I know Katerina?"

"Why?" Murin laughed and pondered. "Why, I don't know why," he brought out at last. "A woman's heart is not as deep as the sea; you can get to know it, but it is cunning, persistent, full of life! What she wants she must have at once! You may as well know, sir, she wanted to leave me and go away with you; she was sick of the old man, she had lived through everything that she could live with him. You took her fancy, it seems, from the first, though it made no matter whether you or another . . . I don't cross her in anything—if she asks for bird's milk I'll get her bird's milk. I'll make up a bird if there is no such bird; she's set on her will though she doesn't know herself what her heart is mad after. So it has turned out that it is better in the old way! Ah, sir! you are very young, your heart is still hot like a girl forsaken, drying her tears on her sleeve! Let me tell you, sir, a weak man cannot stand alone. Give him everything, he will come of himself and give it all back; give him half the kingdoms of the world to possess, try it and what do you think? He will hide himself in your slipper at once—he will make himself so small. Give a weak man his freedom—he will bind it himself and give it back to you. To a foolish heart freedom is no use! One can't get on with ways like that. I just tell you all this, you are very young! What are you to me? You've come and gone—you or another, it's all the same. I knew from the first it would be the same thing; one can't cross her, one can't say a word to cross her if one wants to keep one's happiness; only, you know, sir"—Murin went on with his reflections—"as the saying is, anything may happen; one snatches a knife in one's anger, or an unarmed man will fall on you like a sheep, with his bare hands, and tear his enemy's throat with his teeth; but let them put the knife in your hands and your enemy bare his chest before you—no fear, you'll step back."

They went into the yard. The Tatar saw Murin from a distance, took off his cap to him and stared slyly at Ordynov.

"Where's your mother? At home?" Murin shouted to him.

"Yes."

"Tell her to help him move his things, and you get away run along!"

They went up the stairs. The old servant, who appeared to be really the porter's mother, was getting together their lodger's belongings and peevishly tying them up in a big bundle.

"Wait a minute; I'll bring you something else of yours; it's left in there. . . ."

Murin went into his room. A minute later he came back and gave Ordynov a sumptuous cushion, covered with embroidery in silks and braid, the one that Katerina had put under his head when he was ill.

"She sends you this," said Murin. "And now go for good and good luck to you; and mind, now, don't hang about," he added in a fatherly tone, dropping his voice, "or harm will come of it."

It was evident that he did not want to offend his lodger, but when he cast a last look at him, a gleam of intense malice was unconsciously apparent in his face. Almost with repulsion he closed the door after Ordynov.

Within two hours Ordynov had moved into the rooms of Schpies the German. Tinchen was horrified when she saw him. She at once asked after his health and, when she learned what was wrong, at once did her best to nurse him.

The old German showed his lodger complacently how he had just been going down to paste a new placard on the gate, because the rent Ordynov had paid in advance had run out, that very day, to the last farthing. The old man did not lose the opportunity of commending, in a roundabout way, the accuracy and honesty of Germans. The same day Ordynov was taken ill, and it was three months before he could leave his bed.

Little by little he got better and began to go out. Daily life in the German's lodgings was tranquil and monotonous. The old man had no special characteristics: pretty Tinchen, within the limits of propriety, was all that could be desired. But life seemed to have lost its colour for Ordynov for ever! He became dreamy and irritable; his impressionability took a morbid form and he sank imperceptibly into dull, angry hypochondria. His books were sometimes not opened for weeks together. The future was closed for him, his money was being spent, and he gave up all effort, he did not even think of the future. Sometimes his old feverish zeal for science, his old fervour, the old visions of his own creation, rose up vividly from the past, but they only oppressed and stifled his spiritual energy. His mind would not get to work. His creative force was at a standstill. It seemed as though all those visionary images had grown up to giants in his imagination on purpose to mock at the impotence of their creator. At melancholy moments he could not help comparing himself with the magician's pupil who, learning by stealth his master's magic word, bade the broom bring him water and choked himself drinking it, as he had forgotten how to say, "Stop." Possibly a complete, original, independent idea really did exist within him. Perhaps he had been destined to be the artist in science. So at least he himself had believed in the past. Genuine faith is the pledge of the future. But now at some moments he laughed himself at his blind conviction, and—and did not take a step forward.

Six months before, he had worked out, created and jotted down on paper, a sketch of a work upon which (as he was so young) in non-creative moments he had built his most solid hopes. It was a work relating to the history of the church, and his warmest, most fervent convictions were to find expression in it. Now he read over that plan, made changes in it, thought it over, read it again, looked things up and at last rejected the idea without constructing anything fresh on its ruins. But something akin to mysticism, to fatalism and a belief in the mysterious began to make its way into his mind. The luckless fellow felt his sufferings and besought God to heal him. The German's servant, a devout old Russian woman, used to describe with relish how her meek lodger prayed and how he would lie for hours together as though unconscious on the church pavement . . .

He never spoke to any one of what had happened to him. But at times, especially at the hour when the church bells brought back to him the moment when first his heart ached and quivered with a feeling new to him, when he knelt beside her in the house of God, forgetting everything, and hearing nothing but the beating of her timid heart, when with tears of ecstasy and joy he watered the new, radiant hopes that had sprung up in his lonely life—then a storm broke in his soul that was wounded for ever; then his soul shuddered, and again the anguish of love glowed in his bosom with scorching fire; then his heart ached with sorrow and passion and his love seemed to grow with his grief. Often for hours together, forgetting himself and his daily life, forgetting everything in the world, he would sit in the same place, solitary, disconsolate; would shake his head hopelessly and, dropping silent tears, would whisper to himself—

"Katerina, my precious dove, my one loved sister!"

A hideous idea began to torment him more and more, it haunted him more and more vividly, and every day took more probable, more actual shape before him. He fancied—and at last he believed it fully—he fancied that Katerina's reason was sound, but that Murin was right when he called her "a weak heart." He fancied that some mystery, some secret, bound her to the old man, and that Katerina, though innocent of crime as a pure dove, had got into his power. Who were they? He did not know, but he had constant visions of an immense, overpowering despotism over a poor, defenceless creature, and his heart raged and trembled in impotent indignation. He fancied that before the frightened eyes of her suddenly awakened soul the idea of its degradation had been craftily presented, that the poor weak heart had been craftily tortured, that the truth had been twisted and contorted to her, that she had, with a purpose, been kept blind when necessary, that the inexperienced inclinations of her troubled passionate heart had been subtly flattered, and by degrees the free soul had been clipt of its wings till it was incapable at last of resistance or of a free movement towards free life . . .

By degrees Ordynov grew more and more unsociable and, to do them justice, his Germans did not hinder him in the tendency.

He was fond of walking aimlessly about the streets. He preferred the hour of twilight, and, by choice, remote, secluded and unfrequented places. On one rainy, unhealthy spring evening, in one of his favourite back-lanes he met Yaroslav Ilyitch.

Yaroslav Ilyitch was perceptibly thinner. His friendly eyes looked dim and he looked altogether disappointed. He was racing off full speed on some business of the utmost urgency, he was wet through and muddy and, all the evening, a drop of rain had in an almost fantastic way been hanging on his highly decorous but now blue nose. He had, moreover, grown whiskers.

These whiskers and the fact that Yaroslav Ilyitch glanced at him as though trying to avoid a meeting with an old friend almost startled Ordynov. Strange to say, it even wounded his heart, which had till then felt no need for sympathy. He preferred, in fact, the man as he had been— simple, kindly, naïve; speaking candidly, a little stupid, but free from all pretensions to disillusionment and commonsense. It is unpleasant when a foolish man whom we have once liked, just on account of his foolishness, suddenly becomes sensible; it is decidedly disagreeable. However, the distrust with which he looked at Ordynov was quickly effaced.

In spite of his disillusionment he still retained his old manners, which, as we all know, accompany a man to the grave, and even now he eagerly tried to win Ordynov's confidence. First of all he observed that he was very busy, and then that they had not seen each other for a long time; but all at once the conversation took a strange turn.

Yaroslav Ilyitch began talking of the deceitfulness of mankind in general. Of the transitoriness of the blessings of this world, of the vanity of vanities; he even made a passing allusion to Pushkin with more than indifference, referred with some cynicism to his acquaintances and, in conclusion, even hinted at the deceitfulness and treachery of those who are called friends, though there is no such thing in the world as real friendship and never has been; in short, Yaroslav Ilyitch had grown wise.

Ordynov did not contradict him, but he felt unutterably sad, as though he had buried his best friend.

"Ah! fancy, I was forgetting to tell you," Yaroslav Ilyitch began suddenly, as though recalling something very interesting. "There's a piece of news! I'll tell you as a secret. Do you remember the house where you lodged?"

Ordynov started and turned pale.

"Well, only fancy, just lately a whole gang of thieves was discovered in that house; that is, would you believe me, a regular band of brigands; smugglers, robbers of all sorts, goodness knows what. Some have been caught but others are still being looked for; the sternest orders have been given. And, can you believe it! do you remember the master of the house, that pious, respectable, worthy-looking old man?"

"Well!"

"What is one to think of mankind? He was the chief of their gang, the leader. Isn't it absurd?"

Yaroslav Ilyitch spoke with feeling and judged of all mankind from one example, because Yaroslav Ilyitch could not do otherwise, it was his character.

"And they? Murin?" Ordynov articulated in a whisper.

"Ah! Murin, Murin! no, he was a worthy old man, quite respectable . . . but, excuse me, you throw a new light . . ."

"Why? Was he, too, in the gang?"

Ordynov's heart was ready to burst with impatience.

"However, as you say . . ." added Yaroslav Ilyitch, fixing his pewtery eyes on Ordynov—a sign that he was reflecting—"Murin could not have been one of them. Just three weeks ago he went home with his wife to their own parts . . . I learned it from the porter, that little Tatar, do you remember?"

THE END

CPSIA information can be obtained
at www.ICGtesting.com
Printed in the USA
FSOW01n2131140617
35237FS